"The first and only writer of whip smart party girl Southern Gothic downtown literature with a heart. A bold new American voice."
Michael Bible, author of *Little Lazarus* and *The Ancient Hours*

"One of the only writers right now who is scary."
Manuel Marrero, Author and Editor-in-chief at Expat Press

"The only good Substack writer."
Danielle Chelosky, author of *Pregaming Grief* and *Female Loneliness Epidemic*

# NOW MORE THAN EVER

Greta Schledorn

dream boy book club
2025

Cover by Sarah Schmitt.
www.sks.nyc

ISBN: 979-8-992-06632-6
Catalog Number: DBBC014

dreamboybook.club
USA

Well, I'm blacklisted from the European Wax Center. I missed too many Brazilian wax appointments and now I'm only allowed to go on a walk-in basis.

I dreamed I was on a beach. All these chairs were lined up by the water and there was a little girl building a sand castle. I was annoyed by her. Looking at three busted ass pigeons on my patio. Starting to feel like I might never have love in my life. I'm supposed to go on a date tonight but I don't want to. No interest in love or relationships or sex. No interest in anything. I don't even want to smoke a cigarette. I don't have the personality for love. It started pouring rain for like two minutes. I don't want to come across as bitter and resentful. But I am bitter and I do resent a lot of people. I left money beneath my sister's pillow once when she lost a tooth because my mother kept forgetting. I gave her $20 that I stole from my mother's purse. Someone has to watch and listen and write things down. But just once I'd like to be the one someone else tries to remember. The problem with dating in New York is all these boys want to be artists and they don't know they're the muse. And they never will be artists. The artist is the one who submits, who lets herself be influenced/moved. I was a messy child. I had dirt under my nails and dolls on the floor with their heads popped off and paint on the kitchen table. I left a trail behind me. My mother used to say I left a trail. I made up stories and sang songs and did cartwheels on the lawn in the summer. I was always picking up snakes and lizards and things. I cried in front of the mirror last night. Maybe I just need a boy to tell me I'm pretty, to show me what I look like. I actually always feel pretty when I cry. I just keep buying things. I feel too young and too old for everything.

Reading some book on cybernetics. Reading Simone Weil. Reading Dawn Powell's diaries. Reading about Fiona Apple again. Reading *Scumbag Summer*. I told him I was reading *The Lover* and he said that can be us, because he's older and has money. Reread *Play It as It Lays*. I keep watching the light flicker on the streamers outside. They're moving in the wind like little jelly fish. Sitting on my patio in the sun in my pink metallic bikini. I got a sunburn sitting out on my patio in the sun. I was sitting in the sun because I thought it would change something but it didn't. I always think God's punishing me for having sex and I can connect everything that's ever happened to me in a way that backs that up. Maybe I can connect the dots. I should write my book on coke. Had popcorn for dinner and a Coke. Did coke all night. Stayed up all night. Chain-smoked all night. Sat outside in the rain. I bought a mango vape. Switched back to Marlboros. Left the office to smoke a cigarette. Bought them at a deli nearby. The guy inside asked how old I was and I said I'm 28 but thanks for asking.

His coffee table was littered with things I couldn't quite make out. A pack of loose tobacco, not that he really smoked. A Juul with no juice left in it. A mini chess board, all boxed up. A lime green lighter and a bigger lighter for his candle which was almost burned down to a stub. He had a crystal bowl in the center with two sticks of palo santo in it. I picked one up and held a light to its end. He said what are you doing? I said I'm lighting your palo santo and he said what? He said is that what you're supposed to do? He didn't know you were supposed to light them. He thought they were for decoration. After that I left. I went home on the 2 train to the L train back to Bushwick. I knew it was over then because of the palo santo and because of who I am as a person.

I don't love this man I just love having sex with him. He's probably scared of me. He probably hates the parts of himself I show him. I invented this whole story for him, for why he is the way he is. Unfollowed him because he didn't answer my text. He's projecting. I felt like he might understand. I keep picking up my phone waiting for this man who only wants to have sex with me to text me. I have some delusional belief that somehow my thoughts dictate who loves me or if I'll get what I want. Now that I wrote that down he texted me so maybe my thoughts do dictate reality. I'm not interested. I just really don't care. I don't care who likes it or doesn't like it. Why do I care? I keep having glimpses of ideas but not writing them down. On the drive home we talked about boys. I said I'm getting really tired of feeling this like void all the time and she was like yeah dude. He said you're doing what a lot of people think they're doing but you're actually doing it. I don't know what the fuck I'm doing. He said I have OCD and trauma. She said you believe everything that man says and I said what's that disease? and she said being a dumb bitch. She said this thing about how after her rape she got really skinny because she saw her body as bait. I said stop mistaking my kindness for weakness. He said stop mistaking my weakness for kindness. It's kind of the same thing. I said I want a boyfriend and he said and what are you gonna do when you get a boyfriend and the void's still there? Turn to Jesus? I don't want to work hard but I still want money. No one's making any money. Money, fame, beautiful things. It's going to happen either way so you might as well make money. I never want to go outside again. Getting to the source, whatever that is. It's about instincts. It's all about instincts. I can only follow my instincts. I often feel like I don't but I do. I just feel like I'm running out of time. I want to see what comes up naturally. Waking up with the vague sense that I've done something wrong. The internet is finally starting to bore me. I need to pay rent before it's late. Walked past a Cybertruck that said born ready on the side. Everything's a joke. Everything has always been pretty much exactly the same as it is now I would imagine. There's love and violence and money and people who have it and people who don't.

Now I'm here, laying in bed and wondering what the point of anything is. I just really don't care and I really don't like these people. I had strange dreams last night. Dreams about sex and going somewhere. Two things I'm not doing. I want to fall in love. I'm alone like I deserve to be. How beautiful it must feel, to fall into the water and float. He's confused because I did let him control me and now I don't. I'm on a perpetual summer vacation because I never do anything. I open my laptop, I fill out my timesheets, then I go to parties and I drink and do blow and walk home right before the sun comes up. Then I sleep and eat and do it all again. We're all doing this. We're all doing jobs that we don't care about then buying clothes and going out. Some people have some delusions of fame or notoriety or even money but I don't. I don't want anything, I just want to live.

We sat at Central Park and talked about the Bible. He asked what I was writing. I said I guess it's sort of autofiction. He said what isn't? Beside us a group of women sat on a blanket and lace pillows under pink umbrellas and a wooden table, a whole table that they brought themselves, set for a picnic with food and plates and white flowers. He turned on a song by Perfume Genius. A sad song, but we played it in the sunlight. He looked at the women, sitting around the table. He said don't they know we're all gonna die? Then he laughed and rolled a cigarette and smoked it and then rolled another. The picnic people eventually stood up and left and a crew came to pick up the picnic. They wrapped up the food and stacked up the plates and folded up the table and put it all in this big cart that they rolled away. He asked me what my shoes were. I said they're Salomons. He said that's cool. He said those are cool shoes. And then we left and got on the train.

We went to a reading at Earth. We sat on the floor while everyone read. We went to the Comme des Garçons party at Ella Funt. Everyone looked pretty and I felt weird. I didn't know we were going. I didn't like what I wore. We went to see Middle Part play at Union Pool. We did mushrooms and danced. We said we're at Coachella. She said she's talking to four famous DJs. One of them's flying her out to Tokyo. I'm talking to no one. I have no rotation. I want to fall in love in a crazy way. I want to get away. I want passion and romance. I want someone who will fuck me hard and fight with me and understand me and inspire me. I do feel like I got out of a cult. Had weird dreams. Something about fucking this man and needing him to cum in a bag of ice for some reason. I fell in love with him based on his Letterboxed reviews. I have to stop doing things like this. The wind is loud outside like there's a storm but there's not. It's just the wind. Wind is just the air. I think? Looking up what wind is. Went to my old agency's summer party. They're still doing advertising. They're still doing tons of blow. We stood outside the bar when it closed and we talked while we waited for our cars. Someone asked about the agency's stance on Palestine, because it wasn't clear. What's clear to me is that it doesn't matter. What matters is that they get money from clients so they can pay their employees so their employees can pay their rent and buy the things the clients sell. I realized it doesn't matter what anyone believes. It's never mattered but now I've realized it. It's over for corporate America. It's been over. She said money is the root of all evil. I said money is the root of everything. Everything's evil so you might as well have money. We ate lemon pasta and heirloom tomatoes. We went to Victoria and took mushrooms. We split steak frites and I had a beer. I wore my little slut braids. We walked over the Williamsburg Bridge. We ate a steak and ravioli. We ate a kale caesar salad and mozzarella sticks. I'm drinking a Diet Coke from the fridge that was free. Got a cappuccino and ham and butter on a baguette. Made a salad: cucumbers and radishes and feta and fresh dill. We had radishes and butter. The radishes looked like little watermelon slices. Had a beet salad. Ordered McDonald's. Left without eating. We went to Left Hand Path. I drank a blood orange margarita. Drank a dirty martini. Drank a bad martini. Ate a bunch of olives. We had oysters and a cheese plate. Drank a bottle of wine alone for no reason. I want to leave New York. It's too expensive. It's too tough and ugly. I don't want to do anything except lay in bed and watch reality tv. It's getting old and starting to feel end-less. I dreamed I was writing a postcard to some guy who fucked me over. I have too much shit. I want new thoughts. Last night there was a thunderstorm. Some people are idiots and it can't be helped. I ate yogurt with peaches and peanut butter toast.

Got a pedicure then made dinner. Sometimes I feel very evil. Made salmon and couscous and vegetables. Chewing it now. Crazy how much of life is just chewing. My jaw hurts from clenching my teeth so tightly. I'm sitting in total silence. I tripped on the sidewalk and fell on my face. I busted my knee open and broke my Jeffrey Campbell wedges. Have spent most of the summer watching *Love Island*. I started crying over basically nothing. I basically only feel bad. Dad didn't answer me on Father's Day. I feel really weird and manic. Animals get this thing called zoochosis in unnatural environments where they start running around and around in circles. I feel like if i'm not completely perfect everyone will abandon me. I guess I just have to stop doing that. Sometimes people are just people and there's nothing more to it. I'm starting to feel scared like someone might break into my apartment and kill me. Do the obvious thing. That's what always works.

I hate New York and I want to leave. And I want to die. And I want every man I've ever slept with to walk into traffic. I don't want to go outside and I don't want to look at anymore screens. I want to stare at the ocean without blinking. I want to watch a wave after a wave after a wave. There's a spider web next to me. I'm on my patio and it's on the gate. I went to take a picture of it but it wouldn't show up because of how thin the web is. But the wind is blowing and the web is moving, it's moving rather violently, but it doesn't detach. It's just stuck there by two tiny little threads on either side. There's a desert rose stone on my windowsill that I bought in Arizona. I want to feel the weight of a man on my body. I want to get fucking railed. I don't need to obsess over a man in order to live. Decided I don't have trauma anymore. I can do whatever I want and it will be fine. Not posting. Not going out. I feel at peace now. That's not true. But no one can get to me this way, when I'm in my room. I laid out in the sun and burned my face. I rolled over onto my stomach. A blue jay kept landing on the railing with twigs and leaves in its beak then flew away up to the roof. It's building a nest.

Poor people believe in God to cope with being poor and rich people believe in God to cope with being rich. It's hard to stay out of the fray. It's a tough city and it toughens you in ways nobody asked for. I loved him because I felt like he might understand. I don't actually think I'm better than anyone. I know all of my superiority is just deep insecurity. I feel stressed in a paralyzing way so often, from such seemingly innocuous things. From daily life. Going to the grocery store, going into the office, going on a date, making dinner, texting my friends back. All of it feels like a burden. I'm afraid of everything, even if logically I know that it's safe. I don't know how to let go of that fear. I don't know how to behave or what to do or where to stand. I feel lost all the time. I'm always biting my tongue trying not to say something harsh. How can I love anyone without being honest. I'm not good at therapy. I don't want to say anything. I can be honest with myself. I can always be honest with myself, painfully so, but I'm not honest once I'm out in the world. Now I'm back at home and it's all the same. In a couple years the things that seem new and shiny will seem stupid. People will cling to them in a sad pathetic way. Life goes on. Everything goes on. The world keeps turning whether we turn or not. Last night

there was a thunderstorm. The sky kept
lighting up and the rain ran down the win-
dows in a sheet like a flood.

I'm sick of the pro-ana bitches, I'm sick of the edge lords, I'm sick of men with allegations running everything, I'm sick of the trads. There's a genocide happening right now. Nothing's funny anymore. I can't think of one thing. He said sex is out. Seriously what is anyone talking about. I'm always very obsessed with men who I want to be. Men who I want to steal from, to watch and learn from and copy. Sometimes I feel like I'm the last girl living in reality. I can't stand intellectuals. Everyone's reading theory but I'm not sure why. Really I don't get the point. That's not the point. The point is to laugh at memes. At a certain point it's all the same. At a certain point the thread is lost. If you want to understand the world maybe try living in it. I resent the e-girlification of everything. Everything feels like a cult. Probably cause I grew up in a cult. Jobs are a cult, the scene is a cult, politics is a cult, art is a cult, a group chat is a cult, the club is a cult, getting an MFA is a cult. I don't want to be a part of anything. I'm tired of being alone. I just want to be left alone. We're all perfectly capable of coming to our own conclusions.

I dreamed I was riding horses. I dreamed someone left a vintage Dior saddle bag on the sidewalk in the neighborhood I grew up in. I dreamed I went to this party at an apartment some guy was moving out of. Everything was red. The apartment had a bunch of rooms and intricate carpets and beautiful women making cocktails at a beautiful kitchen bar. We could barely get in the door. It was a tiny door.

Had sex and didn't want to. He had weird manic energy and started pacing around his apartment and talking too fast. He kept talking about how his childhood trauma made him cooler. But he wasn't cool at all. Sometimes you'll sleep with a guy because it's just like what are you gonna do. It's like shooting a deer that you hit with your car. But which is worse, being the deer or being the one to shoot it. I've always felt very aware that my life isn't better because of any pain I've felt. It didn't make me a better person and it's not interesting. Last night I dreamed I was with all my friends and family through all of time and they all started to blow up. There were just these massive explosions and everyone was blowing up but me. The people from *Love Island* were there too. I can't let go because I don't trust anyone else to do anything right. I couldn't crash out if I wanted to. I've never made a bad decision in my life, which is probably why I'm so miserable. I haven't been writing, I haven't been reading, I haven't been doing my job or cleaning my room or eating. I haven't even been watching tv. I don't even know what I've been doing. Just sitting here I guess. It feels like it's too late for everything. I want to be in love. I want to quit taking antidepressants. I want to get in a car and drive off a cliff. Going to therapy, which I don't believe in. I just want to talk to a sane person. Or someone who has the answers, or at least pretends to. It's like instead of believing in God I have a therapist. But I don't believe in her either. And I already know what's wrong with me and how to fix it, I just don't want to. I'm always trying to solve someone. Which makes it about me and not the other person. It's raining. It sounds like pebbles. My whole body is covered in hives. I think it's from fucking this guy. He said I thought you quit smoking. I said I tried but I deserve to have one vice. And he said in addition to alcohol and coke and sex? I'm trying to find a thread. A red flashing light outside my window. The scissor's silhouette against the glass. The leaf that's turning brown around the edges. My left arm twitching slightly. The berry-flavored Celsius that I drank on the train to pilates. Pilates, where all the girls look like different versions of each other but not of me. I said the look in your eyes made me think you might love me and he said what look? I'm not looking at anything.

The sun just set. Now there's all these purple clouds above the city and birds flying over them. It looks like an oil painting. Next door my neighbor is standing on her roof with an easel, painting the sky. We're facing opposite directions. She's facing away from the sunset but the sky still looks like something worth painting either way. Down below me people are laughing together in their garden. They're playing quiet music and telling stories. I feel like he saw me, like he really saw me, and he didn't want me. I'm sick of irony. I'm sick of everything. The stakes are too low. I'm too calm. I need to feel stressed out about something real. He thought I was very cool which is always a problem. I'm a control freak who desperately wants to lose control and I can't. I can't let go. I don't trust anyone to take care of me. I want someone to live my life with me. I start to fantasize and imagine a different life than mine to avoid navigating reality. Telling men my needs. Asking for things. Saying or even knowing what I want. He came over and fucked me again last night. He held me in his arms and slowly pushed himself into me, deeper and deeper and deeper. He talks to me like he's a doctor, preparing me to feel a pinch, telling me to squeeze his hand. I want to fall apart completely. I want to be delusionally in love with this man who's emotionally stunted and trying to manipulate me by pretending he cares about my day. I've always wanted a man to save me, from the time I was a small child. I feel completely numb to everything. Nothing moves me anymore. It's cooling down outside. It's time to lock in. I wanted to know him and he wanted to have me. Well he can't!

I want to be able to enjoy a moment during the moment and not just after the fact. I was supposed to fuck him last night but my stomach hurt so I cancelled. I didn't want to cancel because I felt like then he would never want to fuck me again. Like that's my whole worth, is my ability to fuck a man, offer him my body. Which is essentially what I've always been told. We saw a movie at Metrograph. I started crying at the table in the bar after. He's not good for me. He's just a fantasy.

I want to give him the benefit of the doubt. I should give him space. He came back and everyone went to his birthday party. Sometimes I just feel like if I let men fuck me then they have to hang out with me. Sometimes people are just people and there's nothing more to it. Sometimes I feel like the only way to get anywhere is to make men believe I might fuck them. I want all men to want to fuck me but then I don't want to fuck them, so I guess I just want power. People will always be angry when I write about them. And I don't care. Everyone can go fuck themselves. I have a real life. He'll text me. He'll love me and think I'm brilliant. He said I'm too cynical about everything. I said it's just that I care and I want for things to be different and I don't think it's cute or funny or interesting to pretend like nothing we do matters. I watched a video of a little girl whose parents had died, and she knew they were dead, she said they exploded, but how could she understand what that means? It's so easy to not care and to laugh things off when you're sitting in a nice apartment in a city that mostly lets you live, when you're at peace. Relative peace.

I need to just say what I want from him and get what I need. I want to fuck someone I trust enough to take control. What's the worst that can happen. I'm listening to Fiona Apple. I'm reading the news. Something my father told me when I was young and we'd go to the beach. If you see a shark in the water, you're supposed to swim toward it, so the shark thinks you're the predator and it's the prey. You're not supposed to swim away. We sat on the patio in the rain. We put up the umbrella. We couldn't believe who we'd become. I thought I might be pregnant but then I started to bleed while he was inside me. I want him to cum in me. I want him to love me. I want to fuck a married man. I want to fuck someone who has no idea what I'm talking about. I want to go off birth control. I need to be held and handled. I need a man to fill me with his cock and cum. I keep forgetting to eat. I'm too locked in. I'm thinking about myself. I'm thinking about boys. Instead of working I'm thinking about boys. I'm thinking about death. Thinking about death all the time doesn't make me smarter than anyone but I still do it. It's something constant, something that always happens and always has. I'm too sensitive, too desperate, too clearly broken. Nothing works. I can't have sex without feelings. It feels procedural. It feels like

I'm taking a test. It feels like I'm putting on a show for someone who feels more like an audience than a man. I'm good at having feelings without commitment, without defined lines or specific conversations. It's the men who can't. It's always the man who can't. And so they see you as someone they love or someone subordinate. Peripheral to who they are. They'll refer to us as holes or pussy and they think it's funny. My friends and I don't find it funny. We find it sad because we all want some sort of love or connection and we're willing to accept just a tiny bit. We're all very busy. We all have things to do and places to go. We all have too much work and too many friends and too many parties we're supposed to go to. They're all so scared to show you any part of themselves. I can show everyone everything, which is what makes me so lonely. I cry when I'm sad, lash out when I'm angry. I felt like you let me see you. That's what I want to tell him. That I saw him. That I saw him and I loved him. He said three bumps of coke is a wholesome night. He said I have a victim complex. I said that's better than whatever you have.

I remember being young and writing songs. Maybe six or seven. I had a songwriting notebook and I wrote in it and I cried when I didn't like what I wrote.

I need someone who makes me want to
work. Someone who understands what it's
like to feel like you might die if you don't
do something. I felt something. I wanted to
feel something. I need to feel something in
order to fuck. I can't just fuck a body. I need
a soul. I need a mind. I need someone who
can know me, what I mean. I thought he
could but he couldn't. I guess he couldn't.
I only want him because he's always out of
reach. Of course that's from my childhood,
from years of feeling if I did a good job I
could get love. My father made me want to
work and made me feel I had to. I'm jealous of men. The way their age opens doors,
gives them options. It's not the same for us.
I've felt it in real time, the pool narrowing
as I've gotten older and wiser and closer
to myself, as I've started to make money
and do the things I want to do. I'm sitting
at the office. I put lipstick on this morning.
I changed my outfit seven times and went
back to the initial option. I'm starving. I
can feel my stomach and it's hollowed out.
All the women's shoes click on the marble
floors while they walk. There's a pond on
the fifth floor with orange fish swimming in
it. I feel like someone should name them.

It's 4 a.m. and I'm awake. There's a storm outside. Rain running down the window. I can't sleep. I haven't been sleeping or eating. I'm afraid to live my life. I can feel my shoulders creeping up to my ears. I can feel my body resisting the world. This is all so fucking stupid. I should have been spending all this time trying to find love or learning to love but instead I spent it chasing various men who won't love me, who would never love me. The air in the city felt gross. My clothes stuck to me. My face felt wet. My whole body felt like less of a body. I couldn't love him. I couldn't keep getting on the train to see him. I wanted to be mean. I wanted to throw things at him and scream. I would have a boyfriend if I was a completely different person with a completely different past who wanted completely different things. I'm not myself when I'm with him. It's like I become him, like he takes me over. I know I would have given him myself over and over until I was nothing, until no one was there. It's like I believe these men know what I want and I let them tell me. These men know nothing about me or who I am. Here it is again: I'm trying to figure out who I am without a man reflecting my self back at me.

I don't want to go through life seeing the worst in people. He can't damage me. Maybe hurt my ego a bit. My whole life I've felt there was something evil in me, like deep down I wasn't good. I understood the urge to kill and destroy better than the urge to love. I resent machines. I'm not interested in numbers. In high school I was good at math. This is something that I tried to hide. I've always wanted to be more stupid. In 11th grade my math teacher told me I should take AP Computer Science my senior year based on some math test scores. I thought computer science seemed like something for ugly girls, so I took AP Lit instead. Math made sense to me. That was the problem. It made too much sense so I didn't see the point. It wasn't interesting. There was no path, no attempt to reach something, to get at anything or to feel. It was all just there. All laid out by someone else. And who were they and what did they know? Did a 22-minute pilates video and now I'm not depressed anymore. I'm full of life and ideas and hope for the future. I'm in love with everyone I've ever met.

I've been on my phone all day. Watched *Selling Sunset*. I haven't left the house in two days except to take the trash out. My knee is still busted. I'm tired of dealing with it. And my eyelids are all weird and puffy. I got a story published, which almost felt good. He stopped texting me. I got new sheets. They're so pretty. A light, rosey pink. I wish someone like him could love me. I wish I could have shown him who I was, but he wasn't interested. He just wanted an easy fuck. He wanted the power. He wanted me to come when he called. I should go to this fashion week thing at The Standard. It's an open bar. That could be the cool normal thing to do, leaving the house. Now that I don't care what anyone thinks I can be honest. I don't care if he thinks I'm mean. Maybe I am mean. That's not a crime, that's not the worst thing you can be. It must be hard to love me. It must be hard to be my friend. This city feels restrictive to me. All these metal fences and gates. The vines keep growing over them. Readings aren't as important as writing. Better to stay inside and work than to stand on a stage. We went to the Kim Shui afterparty. I didn't like my outfit. Or it felt like the wrong one. James Charles was there and all these kids from online who I didn't recognize. I want to be more sensitive. I used to be more sensitive.

I feel I've gotten mean and cold and tired of everything, or tired of caring. Sitting at my desk in my silk slip dress. Humans are the ones who make the meaning. To machines it's all just words. We're all capable of making meaning, at looking at signs and processing them, turning them into symbols. Or I guess it's the opposite. Objects become ideas. Everyone at the aquarium today was on their phones. We were all looking at fish through a glass then through another glass. What we see becomes our thoughts. Maybe it's a new way of thinking. A new way to understand language and how it's evolving. Like we're gods, helping our creation, showing it the way and showing each other. You build off what's already there, what already works and is proven to work. I need to go to this party and be normal. I'm listening to Born to Die. My pussy tastes like Pepsi-Cola. You know the one. Diamonds on my throat, treat me really nicely. I'm drinking wine. Earlier I ate ramen. I read Lolita. I need to be in love again. We're all trying to be our idols and desperately failing and that's what makes it good and interesting. We walked past a couple fighting on the sidewalk last night. She was screaming at him and hitting him hard with her fists and her bag. She was wearing purple, light purple, and she said you owe me $250 for emotional stress and he said he'd give her a hundred to leave him alone. Everything feels very over. I wanted to kill myself last night. I went to Metrograph to see *Lolita*.

We went to Highland Park and wandered around. We got ice cream cones from the truck and saw flowers and trees and swans and this little fairy bridge. We drove to a Korean restaurant in Queens and ate tofu stew and kimchi pancakes and bibimbap. Watched *Single White Female* while I ate my dinner. Drank wine and mezcal and a sparkly cosmo. Ate matcha crepe cake from Lady M. I made coconut chicken and rice for dinner. Made the age old mistake of thinking goodness mattered. Did pilates and got a bottle of wine from the wine store down the street and pizza from Fazio's. I have a crush on the boy at the wine store and a crush on the boy at the pizza place. I ate leftover chicken and rice with kim-chi. Smoked three packs of cigarettes in the past 24 hours. We split a Greek salad and a chicken shawarma plate. We went to Tile Bar. We went to Bar Belly and then Ten Bells. Went to Treasure Club. Went to Left Hand Path. Went to Nightmoves. Went to afters at some guy's apartment and everyone wanted to fuck me. I meant to have three drinks and be home by one but I drank a lot more than that and then did coke and then got home at eight and had to just start working. I walked to the library in the sun. I didn't sleep all night. I listened to the new Bon Iver ep. Listening to Frou Frou.

I ate leftover tofu and rice. Date last night with a man from Hinge. He bought me two drinks and then talked about how much he hates his ex for 45 minutes. He asked me to go back to his place and I said no, because he had done absolutely nothing that would make me want to have sex with him and he had no aura and his ex seemed like she was significantly cooler and more interesting than him, and he started pouting and then went to the bathroom for 10 minutes, came back and said I think we want different things and I said huh and he said yeah I'm looking for something more casual and I said ok and he said yeah so I'm going to leave. And then he left! And I just started laughing and laughing. At a certain point I'd rather be slapped in the face because at least that would feel like something. It was 68 degrees out and sunny. I smoked two cigarettes. Didn't sleep. Got my nails done yesterday then went to Kato. We went to Carousel after. We smoked in the little vestibule. Bought coke. We went to Trans-Pecos after. We ate pizza and burrata and a little gem salad. We went to the mall in Queens and I won a little pink fox.

This morning I looked out and the sky was orange. There's construction going on outside. They're turning the empty lot behind my apartment into presumably another apartment and I won't be able to see the park anymore. I didn't remember to do a single thing that I was supposed to do today. I set reminders on my phone, I made a physical to-do list. I did none of it. Buying things to dull the pain. Nonstop thoughts. Not doing anything differently. I can never tell if writing things down makes it better or worse. I do think I'd be a generally happier/better/more functional person if I didn't feel a compulsive need to write down every thought I've ever had and every single thing that's ever happened to me and everything I've ever seen or done. I need to have sex. I need to take care of myself and my skin and make money and publish my book while I'm still fuckable and stop floating around. I just need to breathe. I'm watching *Real Housewives of New York*. I haven't been eating enough because everything tastes bad and I'm tired of it all. My brain feels fried. I haven't been talking to anyone and I feel this intense need to be around people, to be in a club or at a party or a show and to feel some sort of energy but I really just can't bring myself to move. I need a new muse. I need someone I can talk to. I need to be held/fucked. I want to start sobbing and never stop. I accidentally left the door to the patio open for hours while I was out and then I got home drunk and realized I didn't have my keys so I had to climb up to the roof and over the ladder to my patio. I dreamed I was at a party and he was there. He brought his friend with him and his friend brought this guy that I have beef with. They were all sitting right next to each other at the bar. I started screaming at him for bringing him there. I said he's a fucking rapist and I stormed out of the bar. And the worst part was I looked terrible. I had no makeup on and I was wearing a stained white t-shirt with my old white sweat shorts.

I dreamed I kissed him and then I was trying to get somewhere and there was a dead
body. Dreamed I was buying shoes with
my grandma. There were walls of shiny
blue and red and black Mary Janes but my
grandma made me buy these ugly mis-
matched sneakers. Dreamed I was a rain-
drop. I dreamed he was fucking my face.
Then I was in the ocean, on a boat, looking
for something.

I went to Central Park to look at the boats. Some guy is playing an electric guitar. The sunlight is glittering on the water. All these kids are driving the boats. I'm sitting on the ledge by the water. The sun's hitting my back. I didn't shower when I got home because I wanted to sleep with his scent still on me. Being loved has always felt painful and it's never what I want. That's always what I want — to understand and to be understood. Last night was Halloween. I wore a black dress with a choker and my platform boots and Vivienne handbag and then dripped some blood on my neck to look like I'd been bit. What was I taught? To submit to men? To never trust myself or the way I feel?

I went to Sunrise every day this week. I drank espresso tonics. I ate a chocolate croissant, a bacon egg and cheese, a cuban sandwich. After we fucked I went to Mominette. I sat by myself at the bar. I ate a burger with fries and had a glass of wine. We met at Honore. We went to a party at a brownstone in Bed-Stuy. Everyone there came from money. Friday night we went to Basement. I wore my Margiela top and leather pants. I dyed my hair. I put on a smokey eye. We went to Chino Grande. We ate beans and rice and fried tofu and cucumbers. We went to Mood Ring later. He told me I'm too down to earth. I said maybe you should count your blessings because I wouldn't be on a date with you if I wasn't down to earth. We went to Alphaville and took mushrooms. All the booths look like cows. I didn't text him back. She said that's not ghosting that's natural selection. I said if you come from money and someone calls you down to earth that's a compliment but if you didn't come from money and get called down to earth it's an insult. And that's why we have to be bitches.

When I got home I realized I forgot my keys, like I always do, and I had to climb over the roof to my patio to get inside again. On top of the roof I looked at the city and all the lights looked pink and blue and they were spinning like little swirls, like little tidepools in the ocean because I was on mushrooms.

I'm obsessing over men and addicted to my phone because I'm bored. Drinking a green smoothie. I have therapy later and a yoga class. Trump is president again. Everyone hates women. The whole country is cooked. I'm gonna fucking stab somebody. I'm so far past the point of being understanding. Crossed the street next to this little old lady who was hunched over and walking slow, but you could tell she was trying to walk faster, and a car was waiting to turn and the guy driving the car rolled down his window and said, take your time ma'am, don't rush. I always want to hide everything. I was always lying and trying to get my facts straight. Danielle and I talked about this. We said that's why we're good at writing, because we always had to make up little stories.

Went to TV Eye last night. I bought a white baby tee shirt with a red deer on it. Then we went to Bonus Room. It was karaoke night. everyone did the classics. Cyndi, Whitney, Celine. I ordered a dirty Shirley and tater tots. Later, after everyone left, we talked to this boy playing pool. She pointed him out. He saw us both looking at him, we were basically just staring and pointing and whispering to each other, and he came over and sat with us. He asked what we both did. I said I write. He said he paints but he writes too. I asked him what he liked to read and he said mostly old white men and I said I like some white men so he asked who and I said Denis Johnson, because boys love him, and he went on a little rant about how Denis Johnson is about "75% there" and I was like totally. Men always do this, always have to assert some sort of intellectual dominance. He asked us what our signs were. He told us he was intimidated by us, then he tried to have a threesome with us.

We split fried artichokes and a burrata salad
with arugula and apples and pomegranate
seeds. We drank espressos. I drank a vodka soda and then a vodka Redbull. It was
actually a really beautiful day. Sometimes
I feel like I get stuck in the energy of whatever I'm writing. And I'll feel insane and
depressed and hopeless and think nonstop
about how terrible and bleak everything is
and then I'll finish what I'm writing and
feel good again. It's a full moon. Or it was
and now it's going away again. I don't
know. It's getting dark too early. We got
lunch in Williamsburg. I had a bacon, egg
and cheese with potatoes on the side and
then a glass of orange wine. We went to
Hotel Delmano. We argued about whether
or not anything would be actually better if
Kamala had won the election. I said no. No
clue what to do for Thanksgiving. Going
to ignore. We went to Public Records to
dance. I wore skinny jeans for the first time
since seventh grade. We found some guy to
buy us drinks. We went to Happy Fun. Everyone said they loved my coat. I thrifted
it but it's from Topshop. I was like shout-
out Tumblr and Alexa Chung. Thanksgiving. Woke up hungover. We went to the
movies and saw *Wicked*. We cried. After
the movie we went to Martha's for pie and
coffee and then we went to Ray's and had

Popeyes. We went to Lucy's and got pho and then walked home. Everything we walked past felt very beautiful. We walked past a broken mirror leaned up against a tree. I took a broken mirror selfie. We walked past a little garden of gnomes and tiny houses. We got coffee at Honeymoon and looked at this children's book called *Little Princess Goodnight*. We talked about how everything's over and how we have to laugh. I asked June if she'd been reading anything and she said just the signs. And I said oh right yeah the signs. The patterns and the signs and the symbols. And she was like you get it and I was like yeah of course.

I feel like I want a closeness that men don't
have much interest in, like I want to know
everything about them and why they are the
way they are and what they thought about
when they were six and if they believe in
like God or love or whatever and what they
think is gonna happen to the human race.
And they're like can you suck my cock.

I broke my TikTok addiction by download-
ing an app that blocks it until you do deep
breathing or make a gratitude list or whatever. Which I'll never do because I'm not
grateful. Grateful to who? I don't like life
and I never asked to be a part of any of this.

We used to go camping and I hated it. I remember one time when I was little I had this big tantrum because it was cold and my clothes were damp and I didn't want any of the food we brought and I was tired of walking and my hair was messy and this other little girl had gone missing in the woods and her parents were running around yelling Crystal Lee all night and her dad was drunk and we saw this other kid who had a stick stuck in his eye and the snail I found died in the palm of my hand and I couldn't stop thinking about death and I was like I'm never going camping again I wanna stay in a hotel!!! And my mom was like you don't belong in this family. And I was like yeah no shit I belong in a Four Seasons.

We went to Sovereign House for the Expat reading. The guy behind us in line for the bathroom said we should go in together to be more efficient. She asked him what his job was. He was wearing a suit. I said do you work in efficiency? And he said yeah actually. He said it's his job to make sure buses run efficiently. And I said I've never been on an efficient bus and he said you must not have been on any of my buses and I said what are your buses and he said he runs luxury travel buses and I said you don't think I'm luxury? And he said maybe not. Then the bathroom opened up and we went in together and when we got out he was like good job, that was efficient. Then I tried to steal a book from Sovereign House but I didn't want any of them.

My uncle said when I was a kid he told my dad he'd have his hands full with me, because I was always doing cartwheels and learning choreography and performing my little songs with my fake microphone and my fake guitar and playing in the dirt and doing fashion shows and acting out music videos and Shakespeare with my Barbie dolls. And my aunt said and then he just sucked the life out of you.

I should do EMDR therapy or get hypnotized or something. I'm fine. I'm actually fine. I like dancing and I like smiling in pictures and I like taking walks in the sun and staying out all night and watching the sunrise and I like doing drugs and going to yoga and it's not cringe to publish my diary. It's not cringe to do anything. I love rose gardens I plant violets every time someone leaves me, etc etc etc. And I'm not broken or empty I'm just a mirror.

He said antidepressants are for dumb people. He said therapy's for dumb people. He said no one wants to read a book by someone who works in public relations. He said I have a victim complex. He said I have a martyr complex. He said I have a superiority complex. He said I'm a control freak because I like to look at menus before I go to restaurants. He said his friends don't like me. He said he likes to be choked. He said he wanted to fuck me and my friend. He said I have a perfect body. He said I have weird anxious energy. He said I'm too ambitious. He said I'm too down to earth. He said I'm not funny. He said I'm not smart enough to make money off of crypto. He said I have small boobs, which I do, but he shouldn't have said that to me. He said you're not Eve Babitz. He said you're like Joan Didion. He said I'm not a heart guy. He said I need to grow up. He said that I read sensitive. He said that I'm not cool. He said that I'm too sweet. He said I'm not that sweet. He said that I'm too pretty. He said that's a deal with the devil. He said sorry. He actually said he was sorry. He said he couldn't teach me how to love. He said he's still in love with his ex. He said he was depressed. He said he hasn't had sex since the last time he saw me. He said I would never ignore you. He said I seem self-actualized. He said I can't play the I'm just a girl, bonked on the head bit. He said I'm too witty. He said he wants to just be friends. He said I'm never gonna feel fulfilled. He said it's never gonna happen. He said that I don't strike him as a crier. He said it's sexy that I don't need him. He said he feels old. He said he liked my story. He said he lost 30 bands today but then he made it all back. He said I seem like I grew up upper middle class. He said he was happy for me. He said he couldn't sleep. He said he was too tired. He said I look like a deer. I said like in the headlights? And he said yes. He said it's just business. He said he loves my mind. He said I should give people the benefit of the doubt. He said we can keep fucking or I can call you a car. I asked him and his roommate what it meant that this guy made my bed after we fucked and his roommate said oh he likes you and he said it just means he's neurotic. I said I'm a slow reader and he said he was a really fast reader and I said do you understand everything you read and he said yes and I said maybe if you slowed down you'd realize how much you don't understand. He said I'm the smartest girl he's ever fucked, like that's what every girl wants to hear. He said I love you and I said I don't believe you. He said that's so opium. He said I'm low agency. He said I'm a slob

when I spilled my drink. He said they'll
never let you back into SAA. He said add
that to your little list because I showed him
this.

I'm bleeding. I woke up in a pool of blood. Last night did a reading at a gallery. Sunday I helped Cass move. We threw everything into garbage bags and then packed it up in a U-Haul. We sat on the floor and ate pizza and drank Modelos and pulled tarot cards. I pulled the eight of cups, which represents abandonment and disappointment.

Called the robot on the phone a stupid cunt. Watching *Vanderpump Rules* while I write to block out the excess. Made French onion soup for dinner. Went to therapy. Did pilates. Finished my work. Stayed in tonight. I didn't drink or smoke or take mushrooms or weed gummies. I didn't even vape. I read and washed my face and gave myself several orgasms, imagining his cock between my ass cheeks, sliding in and out of me. His hands on my throat. His smile, his eyes closed. Holding my hands while we both cum. Sometimes I just feel like I don't care about anything anyone's talking about. Sometimes I have no thoughts about anything. I'm eating candy for breakfast. Sometimes my eating habits make me feel like a boy. I coughed so hard I almost puked. I didn't write today. People always say to treat writing like it's a job but I don't care about my job and I hardly ever do it to the best of my abilities or at all so I'm treating it more like sex or love or an addiction. Maybe that's naive. Maybe she's sold her soul and there is no love. Maybe I should be making a gift guide or something. Maybe I'm projecting. Maybe he doesn't feel that way at all. I'm supposed to go on a date. I don't want to answer him. Maybe I do. Has an artform ever truly died? Maybe somewhat. This is all very delusional.

God I was so delusional. Maybe that's fine though. Maybe if I did one thing at a time it would all be done faster. Everything's rotting. Had to throw away my lemons and a head of kale. I'm always just writing down the first thing that pops into my head. The connections come up naturally. Patterns form in nature, everywhere really.

I'm putting off going to CVS to pick up my prescription. I can't just have everything hand delivered to me. Things should be hard and take a lot of time. I can't eat. I have to go off Wellbutrin. Everything tastes like dirt. Big pharma doesn't want me to care if my food tastes good. My life is very easy. I'm getting a cold I think. I'm freezing. It never worked to fight with him or to cry or even to storm off and drive away or go to my room. The only thing that ever worked even remotely was to stay calm and not react, which I don't know how to stop doing.

My Margiela flats came in the mail today. They fit me perfectly but they don't change me. I don't want to walk in the rain. It seems so boring, the distance between my house and CVS. There's too much time and nothing to fill it with except my thoughts and music but I'm tired of music.

He was the only person who could think as fast as I can. He was too offline. He was too close with his family. He was indifferent about the genocide. Any time I told him my opinion he'd agree with me. He kept sitting on the same side of the booth as me.

I couldn't get out of bed. I couldn't open my eyes. I don't remember. It doesn't matter. I don't know when it is right now. What day/time. He was sweet and bought me drinks and he didn't even try to sleep with me, then I went home and I'm never going to see him again. I went on a date and he was bad at kissing. I threw away my vape. I've done nothing at work all day. My room is a mess. Dishes everywhere. I left work early to be in a music video for Billy Idol. We all danced with him in a bar. Got a burger and fries and a Diet Coke and split a salad with the table. Ate chicken teriyaki and rice with cabbage and kale. Listening to Nick Cave while I work. Reading the *Futurist Manifesto*. I don't care about the future. Drank a Diet Coke. Going to make coffee too. I'm going to do pilates and then shower. I texted him a photo of my nails after I got them done and I said do u like my nails and he thumbs up reacted. Violence. Rereading *Waiting for Godot*. We really create our own reality. The only way out really is through. I don't know how to live, to live in any sort of moment as they say. Dreamed I was on a yacht with him and his entire family and his fiance. I wasn't supposed to be there but we were all going to the same place.

Ordered potatoes and scrambled eggs and bacon but could hardly eat it. I've had no appetite. Nothing really tastes good. Made sweet potatoes and brussels sprouts and chickpeas. I'm itchy all over again. Probably because I used a new soap. It's natural but natural doesn't mean anything. Nature is very cruel, notoriously. I need to stop thinking my job matters. Money is money. When it ends I'll find some new thing. I've never been good about looking around and seeing what needs to be done. I've never known what to do with my hands. It snowed again overnight. I'm listening to the Bright Eyes Christmas album. Went to see *Carol* at Metrograph last night. My face looks puffy. I need to touch up my roots. Now I'm caught in that loop.

He would always try to do everything right. We'd go to a restaurant and he'd ask me what I wanted and I'd say what I wanted and he'd say that's not really what you're supposed to order here. I'm never going to be able to be in a normal healthy relationship again because everything annoys me.

Last night went to Dyker Heights to look at the lights. Rich people deck out their mansions and then let the poor people come look at them so we don't start revolting. Went to a sensory deprivation tank. The sign out front said experience nothing. I'm trying to stop experiencing nothing. Doing exercises to make my face get muscular to make my cheekbones higher. This is called face yoga.

Went to see *Nosferatu*. I liked the movie. I thought everyone did a really good job. It was scary but also beautiful. There. Those are my thoughts. I just feel like you're supposed to say all that more eloquently and use more and bigger words, so that's why I never write reviews because I really don't feel interested in writing like that. Last day of the year. Yesterday I bought flowers. I dreamed he broke into my apartment and left a mess everywhere, like he walked on my bed with his shoes on and started cutting things up, and then he left a note on my bed that he wrote me. I understood that — obsessing over evil and where it comes from and if it's inside of me. And then obsessing over men and if they're evil and so on. And I did know how it would end and I do think the ending was right. Then I dreamed I got blood all over my sheets while I was having sex and then I washed them.

Driving through the city and there's fire-works going off around me. There's too much of everything. I feel that sense of doom, that sense that I'm missing something. I don't know what else I'm supposed to do. I have my headphones all the way up and I'm smacking my gum. There's a bunch of noises in my ears. They're fast and high pitched and pounding and it's starting to rain. It doesn't feel good to be your abusive father's favorite child. It feels like I must be very disgusting. Or else very, very stupid. Everything he did made sense to me and I liked him. There. That's what I've been trying to explain.

New Years' Day. A man drove a truck into a crowd in New Orleans in the French Quarter. Fifteen people died. A Cybertruck exploded outside Trump Tower in Las Vegas. He didn't answer me last night when I texted him. I don't care about what's in or out. Maybe there is no like war between good and evil. I thought he understood but he doesn't. I don't know why it hurts me so much. Whatever. I hate them all. Suffering is built-in. It's not something that needs to be sought out, but then it shouldn't be avoided either. I've gotten validation before, so I know that it means nothing. Nothing I accomplish will fulfill me. I made cinnamon rolls and eggs and bacon for breakfast.

There's a woman at the coffee shop crocheting a scarf. A million people just walked in. I'm sitting by the door so every time it opens I get a hit of cold air. I feel irrationally annoyed that people are coming into the coffee shop. Some guy brought his dog. We shouldn't let dogs come into coffee shops. I'm like why are you all here, at my coffee shop. The music they're playing sounds like The Shins or something. It's not The Shins but that's what it sounds like. I feel like healing would ruin my work. Sometimes I want to be all peace and love and light, but I like conflict and tension and criticizing everything. Maybe that's healing, to accept what I like to do, which is create conflict and tension and criticize everything. I'm interested in things that last forever like the sun and stars and death. We went bowling. I hate bowling. I hate bowling because I'm bad at it. I Googled who invented bowling. The Ancient Egyptians invented bowling. Most of the time when I Google something I'm like yeah that's what I figured. I'm going to become a genius. I'm going to learn everything there is to know and then do nothing with it. I'm going to start meditating again. I'm going to start crying myself to sleep. I'm never leaving the house again. I decided I'm never speaking to anyone ever again. One time before a church picnic when I was a kid my dad told me I had to change my outfit because I looked too slutty, so I went inside and I put jeans on and a red wool turtleneck sweater and I went to the church picnic and sat in the sun all afternoon in the ninety-degree heat and refused to talk to anyone or eat anything. I'm interested in LIFE and LOVE and HUMANITY.

And the thing is, half the reason I even got the job that I have was so I could date whoever I wanted and not have to care if they had any money. But the thing is men actually fucking crash out if you have more money than them. If you have money and they don't. Boys with money bore me. I don't want to date someone like me. I want to date someone who brings out another side of me, the side I feel I lost.

It was crowded and hot and everyone was bad at writing. It was offensive. The quality, not the content. It hurt me. Physically, spiritually, emotionally, psychically…it pained me. It closed my third eye.

I was hanging out with a bunch of 22-year-olds last night and feeling ancient. When I was 22, I was acting like I was 45 and living with my boyfriend and cooking dinner for him. Which was insane. That's insane. And he didn't even like it. I'd cook and he'd be like I want to order takeout. I'm not a wife. I'm not trad. I can't cook and I don't like to.

Started reading *Notes from Underground* in the middle of a meeting today. No clue what these people are talking about. There's a merger. The CEO said everyone tied to revenue-generating activity is safe. He said "you're gold." Everything's mad data-driven. They're changing the name of my team and our titles to protect us from AI. They won't say that but that's what they're doing. We're not writers or editors, we're strategists. We're in-culture. We have fingers on all the pulses. I don't think anyone here has their finger on anything. They said be innovative…be more creative…they said social media is turning into avant-garde experimental video stuff.

Saw *The Last Showgirl* at Angelika. It was like no one there had ever been to a movie theater before. Everyone was spilling their drinks and sitting in the wrong seats. We went to Treasure Club after. I drank an espresso martini and two vodka sodas. We talked about boys and lip liner and our futures. We're adults now. I already had a midlife crisis. I already broke my life down and reconstructed it. I had different beliefs and plans for myself. I almost had a husband. Nobody in this city understands that. That I was going to get married and have babies and be a wife and a mom and live in a house. I never thought about having a job. I never even wanted to live in the city. I moved to the city when I realized I needed a job because this seemed like the place people went to get jobs.

Maybe I should think about someone other than myself. I want to go back to sleep. I want to be in love. I realized I don't belong there. My hair looks amazing. I gave myself a perfect blow out. I feel manic because I'm doing nothing with my life. I'm wasting my life. I'm running out of time and I'm wasting my life. So I'm spiraling because I want to want the life I had but I had it and I didn't want it. I was bored out of my fucking mind. I think the way you see people shapes who they are. They become what you imagine them to be. They could become monsters or gods or something very beautiful and rare. I always saw my father as a good man.

What is the male equivalent of sexual assault? Being accused of sexual assault? No, that's not the same. I'm sure it sucks but it's not the same. It's not the same pain. I haven't been accused of sexual assault but I've been accused of lying about sexual assault. The male equivalent of sexual assault is being sexually assaulted by a bigger, stronger man. Then I'd be interested in what they have to say but until then I'm not. Cancelling someone doesn't give you any power. Boys don't care what girls think, they care what their boys think. In 8th grade, this guy used to go around and slap everyone's asses. He messaged me on Facebook once and asked me to send him pictures of my feet. He said he had a foot fetish. I thought that was kind of hot. But I didn't like him grabbing my ass. I liked the attention. I liked that it made me feel I was hot enough for him to touch. But I didn't like the violation, the public display of power. I didn't like that he felt he could do whatever he wanted to me, and the comfort and satisfaction he seemed to feel in doing it. So I asked his friend Sergio to go up to him one day while everyone was waiting around for the bus after school and hit him in the balls and Sergio did it. And everyone laughed and the boys were all like that was a bitch move Greta, and I was like you're a bitch move. The only adult who saw was the ex-cop U.S. history teacher who voted for Obama and chewed tobacco all day and drank on his lunch breaks, and he thought it was funny as fuck.

Men get mad when you write about them and it's like…I'm cementing your name in history through all of time or until the cloud or wherever this is all stored stops working.

I still don't know what I want. It's been years and I still don't know what I want. I still don't feel any closer to finding it. I don't want to go to therapy ever again. I think there's nothing wrong with me. I like my life. I'm chilling. And even when I'm miserable it's because I like to be miserable. I'm trying to find a man to be in love with. This is the problem: no one wants to have a toxic, passionate fling. Everyone wants to either marry you or fuck you once a week without talking. I want to feel insane. I want to feel really fucking insane.

I asked him what mogging meant. He said
how do you not know what mogging means,
and then he couldn't give me a definition.
He said you know, like being mogged. Like
when you mog someone.

I have everything I want. I have everything I need. I am love. I am fun. I have an awesome personality. Everyone loves me except for my haters and detractors. My haters and detractors give me power. People who reject me work have bad taste. People who don't like me have bad morals. My hair looks perfect. My lips are a perfect size. I'm awesome to have sex with. I've never been off-putting. I am real. I am just as real as everyone else is…

This month won't end. I saw him walk in and saw him see me. Went to the Heavy Traffic reading. Went to Treasure Club after. I'm deleting Hinge. I'm getting on Seeking Arrangements. If it's over for love I should at least get money. Went to a billionaire's birthday party and she had an open bar. I drank a bunch of vodka sodas. We smoked cigarettes inside. Got coffee at La Cantine. Had a cappuccino and a sandwich. Took mushrooms randomly. Most of the time I'm trying really hard to pay attention to what people are saying and respond to it. We ate empanadas and donuts and French toast and hash with duck in it and drank mimosas. He paid for it all because he's rich now. He called me a sociopath. I called him a narcissist. We finished our drinks and put on our coats and went home to our houses. He called a car and I walked, even though it was raining. He said why are you walking home in the rain? I said I'm already wet.

Sometimes I'm afraid that I'm not funny enough. Sometimes I'm afraid that I'm too funny. I'm at the office. I did a tiny bump of coke in the bathroon. The bathroom smells like blood. There's blood in the bathroom. It feels out of place. This doesn't feel like a place where people bleed, where they have blood inside them. Sometimes I think I should go back to Florida or the middle of nowhere or Europe or LA, anywhere with nature. But it's more interesting to be a romantic in a city like New York. It's more romantic. There's more to push against. There's more tension, more to resist, more to push through.

Got really drunk last night. He texted me. He's been texting me a lot now that we're friends. He doesn't want to fuck me anymore, I guess. He said he has an ex he's getting back with but I don't think he's being honest. I don't really care. I love lying. I always lie. Usually I lie to spare people's feelings. It's always odd to me that people are so obsessed with being honest. They want to really know honestly what you think of them. I really don't want to know what someone thinks of me unless it's something nice. Did pilates. Going to make salmon and eat it with the hummus I got for lunch. Then will shower and clean my room and then meditate with candles lit and read something. My room smells like a fig or something. My body always feels better after I do pilates but I always forget this. I'm stoned and having realizations. I used to draw fashion designs and magazine covers on the back of my Sunday school worksheets at church. Nobody said anything I wanted to write down yesterday. I miss when he worked at a bar. I made him a playlist once to play at the bar. I asked him to play Total Control by The Motels and he did.

Love presumes innocence. I don't, but
that's what love does.

I didn't sleep at all last night. I felt wired. I have to come to terms with the material world. I wish someone would give me money and save me. I don't want to do everything myself for the rest of my life. I'm feeling concerned about the state of things. Spiraled all day. Got my bangs trimmed. Went to Ichiran alone and ate ramen. Certain things I just can't do anymore. There are places I can't go, people I can't speak to. These are bitter, hateful men. I wonder where they came from. Everything comes from something. People think it's weak to feel pain but it's not. It's the only way to get thick skin, to withdraw and heal and let new skin seal the wound. We like to be confused and lied to. We like to be tricked. Gonna write the 48 laws of power for girls. The 48 laws of girl power. The 48 laws of power, girl. It's all about knowing when to cry and when to not cry.

We went to Tabaré and ate pasta and a salad with endives and pears. Drank two glasses of wine. We went to Elsewhere and Jupiter Disco and then took a car to the city. I drank a vodka Redbull. Went to 169. I asked the bartender to charge my phone. Last night went to the Grailed party at Nublu. Everyone was fucking annoying. We went to Funny Bar and drew pictures on the table. They made us check our coats. They were being very serious about us checking our coats. They told the people behind us to leave because they were at capacity but when we went in it was empty. I only had one drink the whole night cause I woke up still drunk that morning.

He said so you're a writer? and I said yeah, and he said I love writers and I said really? and he said yeah and I said all of them? and he said yeah, and I said that's crazy and he said why is that crazy and I said I can't stand a single one of them.

We made out but I didn't feel like fucking him. I got home at 6:30 this morning. Called out of work. I can't remember the last time I slept next to a man. Actually I can. We had insane amazing sex and then he left in the morning and we never spoke again. He came over last night and fucked me. I want to fuck him forever. I don't want to be alone forever. I blocked his number and I'm never speaking to him again.

I told him I'd looked into getting an MFA, but I didn't want to fill out any forms. He said I should get AI to do it, and I said that feels like the same thing as filling out a form. We were sitting on the couches at his office. I was tipsy from mimosas at brunch. I went to turn on the heat and the labels on the circuit breaker said heat front and heat back. I said whats the front and the back? And he said the front of the room and the back of the room. And I said but which is the front and which is the back? He said the front is the side that faces the street. He said what else would it be? I said I think it depends on how the furniture's arranged. He said what's the front of a plane? I said the direction it moves in. He said it's the side that looks out. The front of a theater is the screen. It's what you can see. I think humans will go extinct and pass along our knowledge to some sort of cyborg. I'm interested in the moment right before. The moment right before death, right before one thing ends and the next begins. That's always the most beautiful moment. As a child I'd imagine terrible tragedies and watch myself sob in the mirror. It's emotional pain I enjoy, not physical. I don't want to be tortured. I don't even want to go for a run. I just want to imagine death and destruction.

It's not that I have a problem with sexting. I'm just tired of everyone saying everything in an ugly way. I don't want to text someone a pic of my tits. I want to send him a photo of my breasts, which cover my heart… there's actually no good word for tits. Tits is the prettiest one. I'll send him a nude. A topless photo. A photo of my nipples, pink behind sheer fabric. Tits just reminds me of a cow…there needs to be a word for tits that doesn't remind me of milk. Maybe it's not that these words are ugly, just that they're mundane. They're the easiest words that come to mind. Sex I guess is mundane. But it's not to me. It's always been elevated. To me it's some holy glowing thing, like art or something. Everything changes me too much. And it is like that every time for me, if it's good, if I sort of love the person. It's never mundane to me. Never like a bowl of cereal or brushing my teeth or something.

He came over and fucked me. He fucked me like he loved me. He told me he liked that I hadn't shaved. I asked him if he missed fucking me while I was fucking him and he nodded his head. He grabbed my hands and cupped my face. My nails were done. I had them red. He texted me to say happy Valentine's Day. I said you can't do that. You can't just keep disappearing and he said he was sorry, he said that's never his intention, but that doesn't change anything. He got up to leave that night and it was only 10:30. He said that's so early. I said there's still so much time left and he said so much time and then he kissed my forehead and went home.

Luigi Mangione is the perfect example of why it matters so much to be hot. If he was ugly he wouldn't have half the support he does or people would say he's a murderer because he's bitter and ugly. If you're hot you can say whatever you want. You can kill someone. And even if people don't like it, they can't say it's cause you're ugly.

I don't feel like reading or writing or talking to anyone or getting out of bed. I don't even want to drink water. I feel annoyed that I have to drink water. I have to get my nails done later. I don't get the point of doing any of this. It feels like everything is ending/over. It feels pointless to do anything. It feels like everything is collapsing, or on the verge of. I should put more money into crypto. I should stop buying clothes. I should go on dates with boys who like me. I've only ever been motivated by men and love. By men who don't love me. The wifi is out so I can't do my pilates video. I'm not keeping up with the things I should keep up with. He thinks I'm an actual idiot. I don't even know which man I'm talking about specifically. I want a cigarette or a vape. I haven't smoked or vaped in four days. Mainly because I couldn't get out of bed for four days but that's beside the point. My therapist said if smoking gets me out of the house it's fine. I saw a tweet that was like when people say they smoke to go outside it's like saying Pavlov's dogs ate because they liked the way the bells sounded. Anyway I did leave my house and I got my nails done and it wasn't that bad and it was sunny.

I'm too old to be this avoidant. I can't be vulnerable. I can't tell anyone how I feel. Or I can't really tell how I feel. Or I think how I feel is stupid and not important. People like controversy…I always forget this. I always forget what people like because I don't usually like it. I literally like when everything's nice but it never is and I can't ignore it. I can't pretend everything's nice when it's not.

In Providence. New York has fried my brain. Asked a guy for a cigarette outside the restaurant and he gave me two. He said take as many as you want and handed me the pack. He was cute but I couldn't abandon my friends and I don't live there. Jamin said you underestimate how far a man will travel for a girl. I said not in New York City. Here they're like oh sorry you live in Bushwick that's too far. Because they're pussies. He said he pierced his brother's septum with a nail when they were young. Then he said I don't think I did it right though and we were all like yeah surely not. I cooked charred cabbage. He said he made lobster, that he got it from a tank in a grocery store. I said I used to love looking at the lobsters at the grocery store when I was a kid. I thought they were there to get adopted like at a pet store. I said I thought they were there to get loved and cared for but they were there to get eaten. We ate lobster rolls and a seafood tower. We had crab dip and a big Greek sal-ad which we shared. I got a Diet Coke and it was flat. I had scrambled eggs and sausage and rye toast. We shared some sort of broth with mussels in it and bok choy I think. I had a martini and a drink with mezcal and lemon.

I don't know what I'm doing with my life. I need a new laptop. I need a new job. I need to finish my novel. I need to fall in love. I guess I want to prove I'm worthy of love more than I want to be loved. He said it'd be easier to get a boyfriend once I have a book out. I said I don't think it works that way for women. He said I couldn't get a boyfriend if I tried. But I could. I could get a boyfriend if I tried.

I'm so tired and I don't know why. I slept eight hours last night. I took Adderall and antidepressants and had a cup of coffee and smoked two cigarettes. I shouldn't still be tired. I ate a scone from Balthazar for breakfast and leftover sweet potato and chickpeas for lunch. I'm reading *Hunger* by Knut Hamsun. I'm listening to the 1975. My sheets are wrinkled and falling off my bed. Things can just be fun and interesting and not mean anything deeper. I want someone to write me a letter. I want someone to take me somewhere beautiful. I want someone to make me coffee in the morning. I'm still punishing myself for something. I'm sick of everybody's writing. There's a ringing in my ears. I hear it all the time. There's a truck driving past outside. I looked up why can't I fall in love. Danielle looked up why am I always in love. The internet told us both we have low self-esteem. I don't think I have low self-esteem. I just don't like anyone and I want my apartment to be clean. You should see the world for what it is and people for who they are and still try to love them. Otherwise there's nothing.

I started crying after pilates. The class was a 30-minute hip opener. Trauma people are always saying things like that. They're always saying things like trauma is stored in your hips. It's always sounded to me like one of those things people just say that doesn't mean anything. But here I am, crying after my hip opener. That's what I remember really, the bright blue socks he sent me home in. I couldn't find my socks or my underwear or the backs of my earrings so he gave me a pair of socks and I held my earrings in my hands and I got home and took the socks off and put them in the trashcan and went to sleep. My friend texted me in the car on my way home and asked me how my date went and I said he was sweet and I had a good time and he got me a car home, which I thought was nice. And really it's not a good story. It's not funny or interesting, it's just a bunch of stupid details.

People are arguing online about autofiction again. Meanwhile DOGE is blocking humanitarian assistance. Meanwhile Elon Musk is extorting my agency to get clients to spend more money on "X." He's threatening to block the merger. And it's funny but it's also not good. It's not a good sign.

I'm looking at a spreadsheet and I want to blow my brains out but I need to pay my rent and I need to order eggs off Amazon Fresh because they don't have them at my grocery store. I went out last night and woke up crying. I went out and had fun with my friend and made new friends and I kept hearing this buzzing, this little buzzing at the bar that was in my head. I know the buzzing was in my head because no one else there heard it but I couldn't stop paying attention to it. This is how it always goes for me. I'm always having fun until I'm not, until I start to see and hear things and I can't ever see past them. I remember crouching on the ground outside the bar on the patio while this guy rolled some dice. We played a game with dice. We all put down a dollar. I got cash out of the atm to pay for our drinks. I did the math and tipped. I don't remember paying but I have less cash than I took out so I must have paid. I asked everyone at the bar for a cigarette and finally found one. I looked in the mirror in the bathroom and I hated my hair. My hair looked bad last night. I took a bunch of pictures to convince myself I'm pretty and I hated all of them except for one I posted on my story. I'm starting to blow up all these stories, to turn events in my life into something someone might find interesting. Nothing about my life is interesting. I wake up every day and do my job. I basically never have sex. I'm going on a date tomorrow with a skater boy because he seems cute and like he might be fun. Last night at the bar my friend said fucking these guys is like eating McDonald's. One minute you really want it and once it's done you wish you'd had a salad. You wish you'd had anything fulfilling, anything that might make your skin glow or keep you living longer. She said it's not good to eat McDonald's. I said it is if you're hungry, and you can't afford groceries and the store doesn't have eggs anyway. I woke up and ate Popeyes that was in my fridge from the last time I went out. I haven't been in love in years. The last time I fell in love I felt stupid. I couldn't stop looking for proof he didn't love me and then of course I found it. That's one thing I'll always find. I can always find proof of the things that I believe. I have a lot of theories and I find a way to prove them. I've been reading *Mrs. Dalloway* and I want to feel like her. I want to feel like a woman who throws beautiful parties and puts on a beautiful face and presents the world with something to live for. I feel more like the man who I know in the end will kill himself. I feel more like Virginia Woolf. I won't kill myself because I care too much about finding things to believe in and looking for proof of them but I understand the impulse. There seems to be a lack of hope. That's something we all agree on. I feel some vague responsibility to put hope in my writing, to give people something to believe in but it's something I never know how to do. AI could do my job but instead of letting it they're just looking for new things for me to do. They're making up new things to do to keep us busy so we can all fill out our timesheets even though we're supposed to do things faster because we're supposed to use AI to do them faster even though no one can say that we're supposed to use AI. New things that don't matter but I still have to do them so I can have a room to write in and a place to sleep alone.

It's a beautiful day but I don't want to go outside. I'm trying to reframe my thoughts. I'm not crashing out. I'm famous. I miss getting coffee and going to the park. I used to get coffee and go to the park. I can't think about that now. I feel afraid of everyone. I feel incredibly anxious. I feel like I have nothing to say. I feel like I don't have the right personality. I feel pretty normal. I feel like I'm in my own world all the time. I want to merge souls with someone. I want someone else's brain in my brain / heart in my heart. I'm not even sure I like art. I don't want to read anymore. I guess I might be "super depressed." I have to let go of my life, of the need to remember everything. I'm feeling very sad. I feel I can't trust the way people treat me. I feel almost manically happy. Am I in my loser era? No.

There is this sense that no one knows me. Who can a person be without other people? Most of my time is spent alone. No one reflects me and I don't reflect anyone else. I sit at my desk and type or read or lie down and sleep or cook or do pilates. It's only when I'm out, when I'm drunk and on drugs, that I'm around people. When I'm out I want to stay out, when I'm in I want to stay in. That's one of Newton's Laws.

Why do I always think the most honest thing to say is something dark and mean? I'm sitting down to write and trying not to feel afraid. That's the fear — not that I'll find something awful but that I'll find nothing. I'm a lover and a dreamer and a thinker. That's why having a job is hard for me and why I need a patron.

I was a very shy and gentle girl. That's not true…that was who I thought I should be and who I became for a time. I wanted to be loud and the center of attention. I learned early on the consequences of doing what I wanted, saying what I wanted, responding to things naturally without thinking first. I didn't learn the consequences of not doing what I want until recently. It's not "work" that's important, it's just action. Making any decision and walking in any direction. If you're not doing it now you're never going to do it. I want to live in a one bedroom apartment and fill it with books and art and beautiful clothes and to travel and see things and sleep with men I hardly know. It's beautiful to love someone you hardly know.

It's the difference between understanding (the facts, the concepts, the theories) and knowing (how the facts feel). I'm not writing about what happened. I don't care what happened. I'm writing about how it feels. But I'm not writing about how it feels either. I'm trying to write something that will make someone else feel what I felt. Maybe I'm abusive…Someone wrote a tweet like that, about how the hottest thing a man can say during sex is "I know." That's what I'm trying to do. That's the response I'm trying to elicit. I'm trying to get someone to say I know. Or I'm saying I know. I just feel like I've always known…I don't need tough love. I need regular love. Tough love doesn't work. It doesn't motivate people, it burns them out. It makes them less able to withstand the pain of life that is inevitable, by creating pain that isn't necessary.

My diary is my novel. It's the first draft, where I write down the things people say and how I felt. It becomes a novel when I remove myself, as much of myself as I possibly can, and replace myself with someone I invented and make her interact with people I invented too.

I didn't hate church growing up because of what it taught us, I just hated it because it was boring. I didn't want to sit in a cold room for an hour and a half listening to an old ugly man talk. I did actually like the Bible. I liked the verses. I liked thinking about the valley of the shadow of death and things like that.

I can only know my own truth. Because I can feel whether or not it's true. I'm the one who knows. But I believe if I know my own truth, if that's what I'm looking at, then it must extend outside myself. It must be somewhat universal. I always try to write about love and I always start to get bored. I always end up at the same conclusion. It only works as long as you're both committed to the same delusion. Once one person's out, it's over. Is love enough? No, love's not enough.

I'm attempting to describe things more precisely. What things look like. Here's what's on my desk: Light pink velvet Miu Miu sunglasses case, a silver dome ring, a pack of Rider-Waite tarot cards, a tub of vaseline, chrome candle holders with ivory candles in them, burned almost to the wick. A Laneige lip sleeping mask, the one in the pink pot. My current pack of birth control. Above my desk is my mirror and hung on the wall with a thumb tack and a clip, my Jenny Holzer postcard: The breakdown comes when you stop controlling yourself and want the release of a bloodbath. These are the things I can see and touch. That was Lacan I think who said that about love, that it's giving something you don't have to someone who doesn't want it.

So much of what's happening in the "art world" feels very xD random to me. Maybe books can be like merch for TikToks. I'm too sweet. I'm never going to make it. I'm trying to breathe deeply and not be anxious and not cry. Maybe the point is to stay busy and not think. TikTok is very bad for your brain. I'm not looking at it anymore. But then the poet must not avert his eyes. That's why I'm so afraid of everything. Because I'm afraid none of it makes any difference. I'm afraid I could accomplish everything and have all the money and time and books and movies and art and music and parties and food and love in the world and life would still seem just slightly bearable. I start to feel confused by what drives everyone. I'm writing a book basically to keep myself occupied. Everything I write is a love letter. I'm almost always imagining one specific person when I write. I'm always talking just to them. So there, I need a muse. I need a boyfriend who's older than me for wisdom and perspective and a boyfriend who's younger than me who can keep me up to date about what's going on online. And then I want a third boyfriend who's just normal and hot and does fun things with me. Men are muses. I said that to someone once and he got so mad. He said how am I muse and I said you're amusing. He said that's not what a muse is and I said it is to me. But that's really what I want from a man. To be entertained. I'm looking up the etymology of the word muse. It goes back to Mnemosyne, the goddess of memory and mother of the muses. So really a muse is whatever you remember, which is what you pay attention to.

I'm not a victim, I don't see myself as one. I've made peace with things that have happened. I don't get mad that often but when I do I feel like I could genuinely kill someone. And I wouldn't feel bad about it.

Just finished *The Sun Also Rises*. I'm starting to become a serious doomer. I need to get rid of everything I own. I need to buy a new laptop. This is when I wish I had a man to talk to. I need to think less about how he never loved me and more about how to make as much money as possible. Got jealous of a girl I saw online who has the same name as his ex. Because I don't have that name.

It's all the sacral chakra, sex and creation. Men are extremely needy. That's why women who marry rich end up broke and alone — because it's a job. It's business and you need to read the contract. I don't like giving men what they want. Which is actually what they want. They want something to work/live for. A carrot on a stick. I'm giving these boys a will to live and they should be grateful. That's the American Dream. Don't kill yourself, I might fuck you one day. I should start a religion. I could be the first female Abrahamic God. The sun is setting and the sky is pink. The glass buildings are orange from the sun reflected in them. The days are getting longer. I used to fill all the margins of my notebooks with giant overlapping spirals. I feel like a new person. I'm not coming from an ugly place. I'm coming from a place of beauty.

I walked to Maria Hernandez and smoked three cigarettes. I listened to Snow Strippers while I walked in my wired headphones. I stopped at the deli by the park where they sell cigarettes for $10 and bought a pack. The guy at the counter said it's Thursday, and I said we're almost there. To where, I don't know, that's just what people say. We're almost to the end of something. Something's almost over, thank god.

We've made it too easy for people to get what they want. We shouldn't have what we want, we should want it. We should enjoy wanting it. We've turned work and discipline into punishments. It's not punishment to work or to write. It's not a punishment to exercise or cook dinner or walk to the store. Time, more than anything, is what we should value. When that's allegedly what everything we're creating is buying us. But it means nothing if we don't use it. It's like having a million dollars and living in a shitty apartment and never leaving it. What would be the point.

We went to Saraghina and split cacio e pepe and rigatoni and a carafe of red wine. We had focaccia with ricotta too. We went home early, before 10, which felt good and adult. We went to Cherry on Top. We split a bottle of prosecco and a bottle of orange wine and a cheese plate. I ordered truffle fries and a glass of wine and some cocktail with strawberries in it. After the reading, we went to Home Sweet Home and danced. We took the train home. Went to the book party at Gelso & Grand. We went to Funny Bar. I had a martini. I chugged the rest of it before we left and ate the olive. We went to see this girl's sister DJ at a normie bar I'd never been to. I was crashing out on the way to the show because I forgot to eat and the train was late and my shoes were giving me blisters. We went to a bar called A Bar. I drank a beer. I wore my Ganni dress, the one I just got hemmed. I wore my new Margiela flats and a long skirt, folded over at the waist because it was too long, but I liked how it looked folded over.

I shouldn't have told him anything. It feels like in order to make it in any capacity I have to become someone who doesn't care about these kinds of things. Cass said I seem like a new person. I'm like positive for the first time in my life. I believe people can change because I've changed. People can love because I've loved. Etc, etc. I said I really wasn't going to fuck you and he asked why not and I said I don't fuck other writers, because I don't. I said I try to stay out of the fray. And then I fucked him and then I went home. Someone gave me public speaking advice to imagine yourself just talking to one person to calm your nerves but I actually do the opposite and imagine I'm like giving my acceptance speech at the Oscars. And then it's like why would I be nervous I'm Angelina Jolie. I'm beautiful inside and out and my aura makes people think I hold some sort of ancient wisdom. Because I do.

They have no ambition, they have no hope
for the world, they believe in nothing,
they're homophobic. I understand that, the
hopelessness. I just think it's weak. It's for
people with weak hearts and minds, which
I don't have and can't relate to. I mean of
course I can. But at a certain point you
have to decide. If you can't overcome that
in yourself you're never going to make it.
There are men who are true misogynists.
Across the board, they don't like women.
And then there are men who, as much as it
hurts to admit, just don't like you.

I got a colposcopy today. They put these giant scissors into my vagina. I miss him and I want him to come back. I dreamed I crashed out at my job and quit. I want to stay in bed forever. There was a knife in the dream, covered in blood from a hand. Some man was chasing me, or someone, and then he dropped it, the knife, into the grass and I picked it up and set it on a ledge, some sort of concrete platform, so no one would step on it.

I didn't fuck him, I just slept there. Then in the morning, he drove me home. He said he's never had a woman tell him the correct directions when I was telling him how to get back to my apartment. He said something about how he doesn't have empathy for that, for the excuses people make to justify their personalities. I don't feel that way at all. Everything comes from something. Love comes from love, pain comes from pain. I believe that. Nothing good I've done has come from just myself. I want to know why people are the way they are. Not so much as a justification, just so I can see them, so I can try to see them the way they want to be seen. But that's how you get to love, when you see someone and know they know what you know, and know how they came to know it.

At the Myrtle-Wyckoff stop, rows of yellow daffodils are blooming. They look out of place in the cold. The only way to get clients to do what you want is to make them think it was their idea. I should be doing that with men. My friend said that once, she was like, you could be a master manipulator if you wanted to. But I'm really only interested in thinking strategically if it's making me money. Thinking strategically is like driving a car…I want to be wandering around in a meadow. Actually that's not true I'd rather drive a car.

I've never understood the concept of being a fan…like I like things…but I'm not a fan…I took my Depop packages to the post office and shipped them. I got a cold brew tonic and a cinnamon walnut crumb cake on my way home. I can't stand the boys here. I'm not anti-porn…I'm just pro media literacy. I've tried to teach boys how to fuck but they don't listen. They say some shit like you seem like you want a boyfriend. And it's like no I want an orgasm. And I want everyone else you fuck to have an orgasm too. I want to crawl on his floor on my hands and knees. I want him to tell me what to wear. The only way to write with detachment is to have already felt everything very deeply. My colposcopy results were normal. I'm just really tired. I'm trying to do pilates to rebalance myself. I feel like I'll never see him again. I got a bottle of wine. I'm starting to freak out about the recession. But it felt nice to be held while I slept, to have someone pour me coffee.

Did basically nothing all day. I don't care about any of this. We were in love. Tomorrow: pilates, ship Depop packages, try to write. Change air purifier filter. Empty litter box. My avoidance doesn't come from a lack of care, it comes from caring very deeply. This applies to both relationships and tasks. Love too hard/care too much/extreme perfectionism.

So much of what men are experiencing is just deep, deep sadness. But they can't feel it, they've been taught not to, and so they turn to white supremacy or whatever they turn to. They're in pain, so they want to inflict more of it. They want you to know how painful it is. But we do know, we all know, we've all tried not to feel it and some of us never do. Thinking the answer is to avoid it, that the way to avoid it is to reflect it, rather than to absorb it, to cut through it and emerge on some other side.

We think we know more than our ancestors,
who were closer to the source, to wherever
we came from. Are we closer at the beginning of a relationship or at the end? I think
the beginning. In my experience you start
close and move further apart over time.
When you remain close, when you contin-
ue to come together, this is love. Phones
of course ruin all of this, create an idea of
closeness, a false sense of closeness, that
ultimately prevents real contact. But what
is the conflict? What's the conflict between
us? That we see each other? That we make
each other see ourselves? We hold up mirrors to one another and want to break them,
want to smash our faces in.

My brain feels fried. My friends always ask what really happened. Nothing happened. I'm not drinking tonight. I'm going to yoga. I'm sad because I stayed out all night doing coke. I'm sad because I lost a friend. I'm locking in on being healthy. Pilates every day. No club. No alcohol. Minimal vaping. Reading and writing. No spending money on takeout. Eating vegetables. Going sane. Sane mode. Be more lucid. Stop thinking about him. Stop thinking about anything. Do the things you like doing. It's easy. It's literally easy. I'm eating eggs and potatoes on the patio. I'm listening to the doves and children scream at the park, construction workers across the street talking loudly. The apartment building is almost finished. I'm reading the *Absence of Myth*. I read him in college. I read a lot of people in college but I can never remember who said what.

That's what my dad said to us: That you can
either get married or be a whore, as a woman. And I was like no dad they'll actually let
you do PR now.

The last time I saw him was the last time I went home. Spring 2022. He said I love you and I said I don't believe you. He didn't love me like I loved him. I loved him like I was the mother and he was the child. The last time I saw my mother we talked. We drank wine. She never drinks. We both ordered white. She wants to fix our relationship. I told her it's hard since she's still with him. I said he ruined my childhood. He ruined my adolescence. I had no chance to explore. I could have been someone else, I said, but I'm not. I said I was so scared all the time and she said, of the world? and I said no. I said of him. I can remember a before and after.

Everyone wants to sound edgy and detached and cool…and it's like…say something real. The edgiest thing you can do is be fucking for real. It doesn't bother me in a woke way, just more so that it's not actually counter culture. Counter to what? Your upper middle class parents who live in Connecticut and voted for Obama? A handful of successful lgbtq bipoc feminist MFA writers? Maybe, but not to the world at large. Not to anything that's ever happened in all of history. Not in any sort of larger picture. If you want to be trad be trad but then you have to call it trad. If you don't like something you need to figure out a way to do it better. It can't just be different, it needs to actually be better. I am kind of like why can't everyone just get along…

I'm sick of like the way things work. I hate when I'm reading a book and someone asks me what's it about. I never know what things are about. Watching the *Vampire Diaries*. I like how everyone dies. And then some of them come back to life. I should write a book about vampires. Adding that to my to-do list. Write a book about vampires.

Everything's green. Eating an Italian sub. Listening to Bob Dylan. Thinking about my thoughts. They're always very clear and organized. I think in full sentences, never just random little words, nothing detached. I'm trying to turn my thoughts off and just have nothing there. Gradually it all becomes something else, it becomes something massive. The fragments build up. People think the goal is to make it in New York when the goal is really to make it out of New York. The story is the absence of a story. The inability for there to be one. Stories have always been what fills the void, and now there are none. Everyone's too committed to their own bits to see any sort of bigger bit, to cast themselves in any sort of larger movie. We've lost the plot. We've lost every plot.

I guess who knows. What do I know. I'm hot and cold at the same time. Too much to do and I'm doing none of it. I have a hard time remembering what I want. Really I don't remember the things I see online. They don't bother me. I don't hold them in or make them part of me. I hardly ate yesterday and then drank and then puked in the middle of the night. I threw the whole trashcan away. There's still a part of me that wants to be a mother one day. Someone's mowing the lawn. That's not right. Forget clarity, forget the trouble of trying to find a man or a job or ever buying a house. Drinking green tea. I should be making money. I should be a different girl entirely. With big tits and more of a personality. Maybe personality lives in your tits and that's why I don't have one. Looking at flights to LA. Planning my exit. Getting out of here. I mean for now. I guess. Whatever. I'm tired but not really. Thinking of reading the news later. After Paris. After my class. After pilates. I keep forgetting pilates. After my pedicure. After I find a husband. Another thing I keep forgetting.

There's many things you can do. I'm just a bit tired of the discourse. These aren't serious people. I'm only funny because I take everything very seriously. There you go, there's a thought. There was nothing in between. I'm trying to do that more though. I'm trying to turn off my thoughts, I mean, and just have nothing there. I only have sex to stop thinking. We live the lives we live because other people live the lives they live. Everybody knows this. There's nothing driving us except the need to be driven, the need to land somewhere other than where we started.

I like when boys do little tasks for me. Men don't know that's foreplay. Let me feel helpless for one minute. Someone figure something out without me. I paid attention to the world around me because I wanted to see what was going on. I wanted to be like a man. I wanted to be able to move through the world like a man. I wanted to not need a man, to not have to give one my body in order to live. Dates are foreplay, too. When your knees touch beneath a table, when you laugh at the same line. I said that once to him, that men don't know dates are foreplay, and he said they know, they just don't care.

God it's boring here. It really does never end does it. What if I'd been a wife? Gen X was the last cool generation. They got Chloe Sevigny. We're post-cool now. Now everyone's annoying and in high school forever. High school being online. I used to try very hard to not be so sensitive. I don't know now. I have no idea. My body always shuts down and my mind never does. Everything's starting to feel very made up. Maybe we've evolved past the need for words. She said we need to be fucking like men. I said I don't want to do anything like a man. This is all just stuff we made up. I think. I don't know. I don't think I know anything anymore. I don't know one thing. Yayyyyy. He's smart in a way that circles back to being dumb. I'm dumb in a way that circles back to being smart. I don't know anything. But then I know it all…that's in the *Tao Te Ching*. Eventually I'm going to get out of here, out of New York, and go somewhere real…like Italy…and be in love and just vibe and not have to take stimulants anymore. My father wanted to move to New York City and be a writer. That's why these boys trigger me. That's why I'm like this. That's what happens when you don't do what you want to.

I'm afraid of everything but I still do it all. My entire life has been exposure therapy. Things I'm afraid of: living in New York City, being single, almost all men, ordering at restaurants, going to pilates, sex, love, doing drugs, dying of lung cancer, pap smears, texting anyone, checking my credit card statement, losing my job, not losing my job, being trapped in a relationship, being trapped in any capacity, getting pregnant and not knowing until I have the baby, centipedes, that my cat's dying, running out of money, that I'm secretly evil, getting ugly, that I'm secretly ugly, turning 29, turning 26-28 as well, living too long, giving birth, leaving the house, toxic shock syndrome, waiting too long to have kids then wishing I had a kid but I'm too old, having a kid and wishing I didn't, hitting the wall, writing the best book of all time when I'm not hot anymore, a future where I have no monetizable skills, and needing to find a husband when I'm not hot anymore.

Sometimes I start to freak out because I can hear the electricity in all my chargers. Sometimes I miss who I used to be. Maybe I was just stupid. Sometimes I feel like this is all an act. He said he read my story. I said it really wasn't like me at all. The girl in the story wasn't me. He said he wondered when he read it. He was like who's the real Greta? Like I would know.

Threw away my vape. Putting my makeup on. Shaping my eyebrows. Sex is boring to me because it's too easy. It's very easy for me to find someone to fuck. So the value goes down…that's just basic economics. When we were together he said he'd never marry someone who didn't work. But then now he is.

I feel like I've been on this train for my entire life. I've been spending insane amounts of money. A small jet crashed into a residential neighborhood in San Diego. The cars all caught on fire. I don't want to wake up so I won't go to sleep. If I stay up forever then it's always today and not tomorrow. It's always right now.

I'm defined entirely by my thoughts. My animal instincts were not good. Lying, stealing, gaslighting my father, coming up with a plan, finding a way out, telling myself stories in order to live, seeing things in such a delusional way that it circled back to seeing things for exactly what they were. I saw my father as a good man. I thought he loved us and wanted what was best for us and that's why he acted the way he did. And it was. And that's how I became a genius. I'm only fascist about art. There should be less of it and it should all be better. Writing has never been about anything to me other than just a way to take my thoughts out of my head and put them somewhere else so I can move on with my life. Not that I've ever done that. The last thing the world needs is another writer. What the world actually needs is doctors and lawyers and teachers and people who actually hold everything together. Everything's just barely being held together...People who don't believe in modern medicine have never had a migraine. People writing about how tech is evil and phones are evil and the internet is evil and then posting it online. People always get mad when I write about them and I'm just happy they read it!

I've always had talent so I've always known it doesn't matter. I don't care about being hot so men will want to fuck me I care about being hot so men will read my writing. It all just sort of feels like nonsense. I'm interested in what's on the surface. I should've been a surgeon. I'm cold and detached and I liked dissecting things in middle school and I'm not really squeamish and I can't get myself to do anything unless I think someone might die. But I wouldn't be able to deal with the lights. It's a lot of fluorescent lighting.

I can never tell if my sensitivity is a strength or a weakness. I used to think weakness. I used to try very hard to not be sensitive. I don't know now. I have no idea. As I've gotten older I've become more sensitive to things that feel good, instead of just to things that feel bad. A lot of it is just physical though. The sun hurts my eyes. Everything makes me itchy. Alcohol makes me vomit, leaves me bedridden the next day half the time. Sometimes when people touch me it does feel like nails on a chalkboard. These aren't things I can control. I've always hated being sensitive, not for the effect it has on me personally, but because I think it makes me less fuckable. I felt the same way about being smart, about being shy, about being slow to warm around new people. Don't flirt with me unless I've known you for at least two years or I'll feel cornered. And then the opposite: mentally I love people. Mentally I want to fuck people. Physically not. Physically I can't feel it. Or I feel like my body shuts down.

Sometimes I think I have no trauma. I think trauma's not even real. I think I've dealt with everything there was to deal with. And then some days I feel completely un-equipped to live in the world in any capac-ity. I feel unable to date. I feel incapable of love. I feel incapable of doing my job, or any job, or going out to dinner. I told my therapist about my rape. I said it was giv-ing rape. Maybe we've evolved past the need for words. Maybe none of this means anything. No one needs to read it. No one needs to hear it. We've all read enough. Everything's starting to feel very made up. Love is made up and violence is made up. Maybe we shouldn't have evolved to speak and think. To name things. I think that kind of ruined everything. We shouldn't be able to identify violence as violence when may-be it's just nature.

I'm sitting at the bar. I'm looking out the window through the mirror behind the bar. I'm thinking about the doctor. I'm thinking about fucking him, him holding me, me kissing his neck. I'm having a hard time figuring out the point of anything. I'm telling the same story over and over again. I dreamed I was on some sort of island working for a client. They hated the copy I wrote and I called my manager a cunt. Then the room we were in started to flood from a wave from the ocean. Then I had to find the train and it was in a cave, but the cave was beautiful. Sometimes I feel like this is all an act. The writing. It's real while I write but then I rearrange things, create another image. But which is closer to the truth? The truth is much less interesting. Lines of insecurity and self hatred. Lines repeating themselves, over and over and over, until they become something I can't even stand to look at. Something I have to cut. Something that would be too revealing, too humiliating, too sad.

An incel is a man who is nice to women so they'll have sex with him, then crashes out when they don't. A femcel is a woman who has sex with men so that they'll love her, and then crashes out if they don't. I used to be a femcel but now I just don't have sex. Which makes me what? A bitch?

The world is gone, the one we lived in. I'm trying to understand the future of the novel. If AI can write the way I write. If writing will fall by the wayside. If any of this means anything to anyone. How is AI different from a dream? It's our collective consciousness, our collective hallucinations. The sun just set and the lights wrapped around the gate to my patio came on. Some of them are out. I'm thinking about the cloud, where everything is now. The cloud is a beautiful name for a place to be stored in. Sometimes I wonder what he thinks of me, if he ever thinks of me. I wonder if he hopes I'm well. I wonder if he regrets the years we spent together. I woke up with my arm draped around the hips of a man I hardly know. I wanted him to love me but he just went home. I could send him something, a photo or a meme or a lyric from a song or the song itself. It's so easy to send things. Instead I make more coffee. I drink it on the patio and smoke. I forgot that I quit smoking. My ash tray is full, filled to the brim with damp cigarettes and a pool of murky water. I'm too scared to throw it out, too scared of what I'll find if I empty it. But here's my thing. Are the people who made AI less human than artists? That's human too. It's human to create a monster. It always has been. It's human to try to be like god.

I keep thinking about him. His voice, the
way he sits, the way he speaks to people,
the way he tells people what they are and
what they do, in a kind way, not in a way
that's condescending, in a way that makes it
seem better than it seems to me. Everyone
is however they're perceived. You can try
to control it, to shape it for yourself, but really there's not much you can do.

We got dinner at Saraghina and then went
to a party at Public Hotel. There was a line
to get in to the party on the roof. We told
the bouncer we were on the list and asked if
we could go in. He said you have to ask the
other door guy. Then another door guy came
down and we asked him the same thing and
he said he wasn't the right door guy either.
Finally a third door guy came down and
walked over and we said the same thing.
We said we're on the list and said the name
and he said oh you're going to the party upstairs, not the party on the roof, and told us
to go into the hotel and up to the second
floor. Then the door guy to that door said
we had to wait in that line. But we didn't,
we cut to the front and said again that we
were on the list and they stamped our wrists
and let us in. Everyone inside looked 21.
A boy squeezed past me and said excuse
me love and I was like you're too young to
call me love. Then we had to wait in line at
the bar to get our drinks, which were over-
priced and terrible. We tried to dance but
it was too crowded, everyone kept push-
ing past us, and we gave up and left and
went to KGB. On the way to KGB my shoe
broke. It's the third time the heel has fallen
off this pair of boots. It's happened every
year since I bought them. I kept walking
with the broken shoe because what else

would I do. Inside KGB, we asked this guy if we could sit down at his table. He was sitting alone. He looked like he was in his mid-40s or 50s, but not a New York 40s or 50s. He said he was from San Francisco. He said he worked in UX design. He made small talk with us for a minute, he looked thrilled that we were talking to him, like he couldn't believe it. We asked him how old he thought we were and he said 69 and 69, and then he started taking pictures of us from under the table and texting them to his friends. We stood up and left. We got in a car and went back to Bushwick. We went to Birdy's. We stood in line for the bathroom and then we stood in line at the bar.

And of course there's still some fantasy in the back of my mind that a man will save me. I spent the first half of my life breaking up fights. I took care of people who should have taken care of me. I hate to be needed now. I don't want to do anything for anyone or be anything for anyone. My mother said I was a terrible baby and would scream through the night every night and never sleep. A girl in the coffee shop asked if there are nuts in the kitchen. The barista said honestly there probably are. The girl had an accent, a heavy eastern European accent. She said I prefer transparency in order not to die.

I don't resent him anymore. I'm not sure I ever did. People can just not be what you needed. I wish he'd seen himself the way I did when I was young. This is almost always how I feel about men. I always love them, I always think they're cool and funny and smart and it's always their own insecurities that ruin everything, their own inability to see themselves. Or maybe it's me, maybe it's the way I'm always searching for validation and never love, and never validation from someone who gives it freely, which, of course, is typically rooted in insecurity. I think we're mostly mirrors, and it's only when we can see past that, when both people can see past the glass, that we become ourselves to someone else.

I'm reading *Black Pill* by Elle Reeve, about the incels/the 8chan founder/the right-wing boys. The people who got pilled. It's fascinating. It's so sad that this is where boys end up. I remember boys my age going down these paths. They just locked in on the wrong things. I was on Tumblr looking at pictures of Kate Moss and Alexa Chung, and then I'd try to find their outfits at Goodwill. Maybe I'm really not autistic. I have a different thing…I'm the girl version of an autistic Chad. I locked in on boys and being normal. I read Nicholas Sparks books. I listened to Taylor Swift. I would just get really into whatever the boys I liked were into. So I guess it's good I didn't have a crush on a Nazi. But then maybe if these boys had been really into My Bloody Valentine or Kurt Vonnegut or whatever instead of eugenics they would have gotten girlfriends and not been incels to begin with. I did date a guy who was really into Ayn Rand but I didn't get into her because the books are too long. My friend's little brother got into all of that, the 4chan stuff. We were in 8th or 9th grade, he was a year below us. And it was interesting because he was hot. I mean at the time for a middle school boy he was hot. So he could have had girlfriends. He made fun of me relentlessly for my teeth, for having braces even though everyone had braces. And we were friends in a way for a time. He was friends with the boys I was friends with. But his dad died in a car accident and he had an older sister and a baby brother and he was in the middle. I don't know what happened to him. One of his friends joined the military and lost his leg. I just learned about that recently. I would go to his house to hang out with his sister and we'd talk to old men on Omegle. I remember going to her house before homecoming, taking pictures in her front yard. I wore a black and white dress that I wished was shorter. Then another boy, who asked me out on the bus around the same time. He asked me to be his girlfriend. I said no, mainly because I thought my dad would kill me if I had a boyfriend, which he would have. Then after I said no he got really mean. He's a cop now in our hometown and look at me. Look what I'm doing. Basically nothing but I didn't die.

I only write because it's a way to feel some sort of connection without having to actually deal with another person. But I am very aware that it's not a real connection, that I'm not actually touching anyone or being touched. It's still a performance at the end of the day. It's still just standing on a stage. That's why I relate to the edge lords, because aren't we all just faking it? Aren't we all trying to create a persona? Aren't we all just trying to hide, so people don't see how fragile we are, how easy it is to hurt us? We're all trying to conceal our innocence.

I bought a cherry limeade just to hold it. The condensation made my hands feel like someone else's. I haven't had a real conversation in six days except to ask the deli guy for a pack of Marlboros. He said reds or golds and I said golds and he said I only have reds so I got reds. I can't stop watching this video of waves folding in on themselves. There's a guy in the building across the street who irons all his shirts at night with the window open. He does it shirtless. I make up little stories for him. He doesn't know his son's middle name. He drinks Diet Coke out of a wine glass when he's trying to quit drinking. I feel like a bag of aquarium gravel. Not even a fish, just the gravel. My wax place burned down, which felt biblical. Maybe I'll be a real feminist now. Sometimes I lie about having dreams just to feel normal. I told my therapist I dreamed I was on a plane that crashed in a field of lavender. But I never really remember any dreams. I wake up with my jaw clenched tight. I had lipstick on from a work call when I took the trash out. My neighbor asked where I was going. I said nowhere but I want to look good when I get there. It's been eleven days since I let somebody touch me. I keep buying fruit and letting it rot just to prove I wanted something once. I spilled water on a book this morning. The

pages curled up into little spirals. I dried
it with a blow dryer and felt like God. All
damage is holy if you survive it. My phone
is on 3 percent. I don't feel like charging it.
I'm lying on the floor. I'm listening to my
upstairs neighbors vacuum. I'm listening to
the thunder. I close my eyes and try to picture everyone I've ever loved standing in
one room but I can't see them. Everything
looks blurry. But that's the point. The point
of being here. Being missed.

The lights were blue and the room was filled with smoke. I've been thinking about how we got here, not that it matters. This is where we are now. I used to believe in facts. I used to think that something was set in stone. We're not in the beginning, we're just in the beginning of noticing. You never notice anything until it's already been underway for too long and then it's too late. The beginning began a long time ago. This is the middle. We're right in the middle, like we always are.

Went to the library to return my stack of books. I owed a bunch of money in fines but now I don't. The sidewalk was blocked off where fresh concrete was poured. Still drying. A man almost hit me with his car. He just kept rolling into the intersection while I crossed. Love doesn't make me feel good, sex doesn't make me feel good, achieving things doesn't make me feel good…the only thing that's ever made me feel good is being on molly at the club. He said I should quit my job and go work for some AI company. He said go work for NVIDIA. He said that would be goated. He said my book sounds clouted. He said I sound retarded. He said I'm acting crazy. He said I'm doing a wounded animal bit. There's nothing to do about anything. I already cancelled him. I didn't actually cancel him. He cancelled himself. I said he should come talk to me, and he moved to Japan.

I'm trying to lock in on my job again so I don't get fired. I wanted his love too much. I didn't realize that in the moment. I never realize anything in the moment. I'm running out of energy. I can't handle being alone anymore. Everything is really bad. I don't understand that. I loved that he made me mad. No one ever makes me mad. I'm pro doing things the way I want to do them. I'm pro being who I want to be. I wish it was sunny. I wish I could go back in time. What am I doing. I don't want to have to do all this stuff. Everyone makes me feel more alone. I have good things happening but they're not making me feel good. Why do I not trust anyone? Or trust everyone too much? I don't even know which one I do. I'm jealous of people who had an adolescence. Angry at myself for not trying harder, fighting more, wanting absolutely anything for myself. I thought I was worth nothing. I thought I was completely incapable of doing anything. I'm jealous of people who were precocious. I was something else…the opposite of precocious…what's the word for that? I started to forgive my father when I realized I would punch holes in the wall too if I had to wake up at 5 am.

I'm gonna find a younger man, like 24-25, who's kind of nerdy and sweet with a pretty face…then I'm gonna swag him out a bit and make him fall in love with me. I feel like there was something I was going to write down but I don't remember. The laws of physics.

At dinner we talked about how we never want to get railed again. We ate pita and hummus and a Greek salad and roasted cauliflower and lamb. We went and walked by the water. Everyone was out, walking by the water. We went to Bar Oliver. We went to Bar Belly. We ate steaks and cake and a salad. We went to Sing Sing. Went to Funny Bar. Went to Seventh Heaven. We watched *Final Destination One* and *Three* and ate Thai food. I started crying at dinner because he told me I don't have autism. He said that's the most autistic thing I've ever done, crying at dinner because I don't have autism. Then I showed him my autism test scores and he said maybe you have asperger's. I said I think that's worse and he said it is.

I want to be one of those girls who's always in love with someone. It just never occurs to me. Saw two dead baby birds on my walk. He got married on my birthday. I woke up still drunk and saw somebody post about it and I texted all my friends and they all said the things you're supposed to say when the guy you were with for seven years gets married on your birthday. Nasa said do you feel iconic? I told everyone I was gonna go see a psychic and then I fell back asleep and forgot to see the psychic. Everyone's asking me how I feel. Everyone's saying you should write about it. What would I write. He got what he wanted, she got what she wanted, I didn't get what I didn't want. That's all you can ask for in this life, not getting what you don't want.

I dreamed I was at the beach on vacation and I lost my phone and my work laptop and my suitcase. But I was really just upset about losing all my underwear. Both of my parents were there. And then I was having to work and had to use someone's phone to tell my boss I couldn't find my laptop because I lost it in the ocean. A lady died at the spa in my dream. She tripped and cracked her head open. Slipped really. I looked down and saw blood and a crushed skull. I can't even have a peaceful dream about the spa. I had night terrors as a child. I used to get sleep paralysis and see figures climbing in through my window and I couldn't move. I used to stay up all night to avoid my dreams.

No roster, no man to hold me, no man to have conversations with or go to dinner. I'm all alone. I've been all alone since we broke up, other than a handful of three month long flings I know won't turn into anything. I'm too scared to get attached again. I can admit that. It's too painful starting over. And that's the truth — love is the thing that hurts the most.

I don't like readings because I can't pay attention to what anyone is saying. I tune it all out. I've seen some of my favorite writers read and tuned them out. I can't listen to podcasts or audiobooks or anything like that. I did the same thing in school. I could either write down word for word what the teacher said or I wouldn't catch any of it. Studying never occurred to me. I'd just take the tests. Sergio would steal the answer keys for me. I'd do his homework and he'd give me the answers. You'd think doing the homework would give you the answers but it doesn't. Eventually Sergio got sent to juvie for running an iPod theft ring and I had to just guess. Usually it's whatever answer you haven't already picked that many times. So if you've already picked B and D a lot it's probably A or C. And then it's not that hard to narrow down. They were always asking questions I didn't care about. It was always like what did this guy do and in what year did he do it. I always got straight A's. Not because I ever knew what was going on. I just had to figure out a way to do it so my dad wouldn't crash out, and then in college, to keep my scholarships, and now, proverbially, so I can keep my job. I should've been on Adderall but they didn't let girls have ADHD back then.

Most people can figure things out if they have to, gun to their head. But then eventually the gun stops working. It starts to feel like there's nothing at stake. It starts to feel like the gun won't go off. In a perfect world, the gun goes off. The gun goes off and then it's over. Everyone turns off the lights. Maybe the story is this: Imagine a gun on the table. Imagine the table's not real. Imagine the gun in your hands, which are real, or were real, at one point in time. Imagine pulling the trigger.

Are you locked in? Are you looksmaxxing? Are you mogging? Are you clouted? Are you Chadded? Are you goated? Whose side are you on? Are you in the group chat? Are you ready to Klarna some Botox? Are you taping your face when you sleep? Are you trad or alt right or dark woke? Have you locked down your personal style? Are you wearing your tabis? Did you find a good dupe? Are you at the intersection of sex and technology or the intersection of fashion and music? Did you make any money off crypto? Did you make any money off art? Do you have the receipts? Can you show me the money? Are you fitted? Dripped out? Have you been to the pool at Bathhouse? Have you been to SAA? Have you been name-dropped in a poem or a tweet or a Substack? Are you even on Substack? How much money do you make off your Substack? How much money do you need to get by? How much money does it take to look swaggy? Do you really like fucking or do you just like the likes? Do you just want the clout? Do you just want to be written about? Are you here because you want to be here or are you here because there's no way out? Do you know which photo to post? Do you know that dumps are out? Do you know if you're on the list? Do you know if someone can get you in? Do you know what jeans are in? Do you know how many books you've read have you read the ones on the list were the books you read problematic were they written about online will the books you read make you famous do you know if books can be evil do you know if books can be god do you know if books should be political or if books should just be books or if books should just be words or if words should just be words or if words should just be human if we own the words or if they live outside of us if the words are more than us if the stories we've told are enough if there's anything after this if there's any life after love if love is real or if love is cope if women are better off alone if women were better off before all the rights if men deserve rights if men deserve love if believing in love, whatever it is, could solve the loneliness epidemic if love could save the incels if the incels could save the beautiful queens what did we do to our beautiful queens are you protecting your beautiful queen are you playing the game or are you one of the pawns are you paying for porn or just watching? Is it bad that people are dying is it bad that babies are starving is it bad to put things in categories like that is it cringe to say Free Palestine is it back to be pro life is that archival? Is that Comme is that Celine is that Rick? Is that Margiela or just MM6? Is this making you wish there were more or is it making you wish there was less is it were or was is it me or us is it peace love happiness or is it live laugh love are you laughing? Are you seriously laughing? Which came first: the gun or the table? The girls or the gays? Are you mother are you cunt are you serving are you slay are you slaying the house boots down is your body tea does your face card go crazy have you ever been to Berghain can you even get into Basement have you even heard of this DJ are you an NPC or an op do you even have any ops do you even know that we're cooked do you even know that it's over do you know that you're not gonna make it do you know if you're fund-ed by Thiel does anyone know where the money comes from does anyone know who has it do you know if you're being ironic do you know if you're being sincere do you know if you're crossing a line do you know if there's a line for the bathroom do you know anybody with coke do you ever cry do you ever sleep have you ever dreamed of ChatGPT? Is this anything? Is the void still a thing are The Voidz still a thing is that scene still a scene is your IQ 140 are you a beautiful mid or are you a 10? Are you a one or are you a zero? Did you commit to a bit? Gun to your head, would you get it?

Usually it's whatever answer you haven't already picked that many times. It's not that hard to narrow down.

For a while we were back, then we were over. We were crashing out then locking in. For a while things seemed clear and then they didn't. We went to Ten Bells. I went to Sunrise/Sunset and had a ham and gruyere sandwich. We went to Bar Cornelia. We went to Lil Frankie's. We went back to his apartment and watched music videos all night. We talked about Jeffrey Epstein. We talked about Trump. We talked about the nature of things, how it's changing, the fact that no one cares, the lengths people will go to. We went to Clandestino and Cherry Tavern. We got burgers at Remedy Diner. I took a car home. I walked in the rain. I walked into the street and someone almost hit me with their car. I said fuck you, because I had the right of way, and he said fuck you back and he called me a bitch and then I walked away and he drove away. We ordered pizza. We did too much coke. We went back to this girl's apartment after the party and played with her snake. She had this little snake. I was someone else tonight. I was pretty. I asked all the right questions and I didn't answer any, not in a serious way. I acted happy and light. I moved with ease. I took a shot of tequila. I bit into a lime. I hit a vape and smoked a pack of cigarettes. This is my life. We went to Fushimi and got sushi. We went to Martha's Country

Bakery. We went to Hearth. We split fried artichokes and mushroom mac and cheese and a carafe of wine because it was happy hour. We went to La Cantine. We split a bottle of wine and lasagna and meatballs and a salad. I said I'm trying to come up with a scam to run. I said maybe I'll blackmail one of my clients. I said the name of one of my clients. He said that's not a good scam and I said why not and he said because they'd just kill you. I dreamed I brought my work laptop to Bathhouse and it got stolen. I was trying to figure out what lie to tell my boss about how my work laptop got stolen from Bathhouse. I was gonna tell him I was working. We stayed up all night and packed up my apartment. We drank and watched the sunrise. The movers came and took everything away. It's not hard to face the terrible ugly things in the world, it's hard to face the good things on the other side of all that. It's hard to see the two side-by-side. It is what it always has been, now more than ever. I'm watching *Sex and the City*. I'm reading *Delta of Venus*. I'm reading *We Were the Mulvaneys*. I'm reading Baudrillard. I have no upstairs neighbors. I've never drank a cherry limeade. But who would know. Who could possibly know. Maybe these things are real. Maybe they're not. How could anyone know if I wrote this or if it was written by a machine. How could anyone know what really happened. Finally got a Brazilian, which always makes me feel like more of a woman, because of the pain. We got dinner at Jean's before the party. We split pasta and salads and shrimp cocktail. I drank two martinis. After dinner we ate dessert. We ordered gelato and a bottle of champagne. We took espresso shots and then we went downstairs to where the party was and danced.